WHAT DO YOU DO WITH A GIRL LIKE SHELLEY?

If you're like her mother, you try to get rid of her. If you're like the boys in the street, you try to use her in return for the acceptance she craves. If you're like the smooth operators in New York's East Village, you try to fill her with drugs and exploit the youth and beauty of this homeless runaway. If you're a dedicated psychologist like Jeff Olsen, you'll try almost anything to reach her even though you know you'll probably fail. If you're like the police and the state correctional authorities, you try to break her spirit and finally just lock her up out of sight when she refuses to fit into "the system."

If you're a reader,
you'll never forget her . . .

"A touching, poignant story about the absolutely unbelievable strength and beauty of a human being . . . even when tested beyond endurance."—Eda Le-Shan

Family counselor and moderator of *How Your Children Grow*

SIGNET Books You'll Want to Read

RUN, Shelley, Run!

Gertrude Samuels

Ⓞ
A SIGNET BOOK
NEW AMERICAN LIBRARY

TIMES MIRROR

This is an authorized reprint of a hardcover edition published by Thomas Y. Crowell. Published simultaneously in Canada by Fitzhenry & Whiteside Limited, Toronto.

Library of Congress Catalog Card Number: 73-12310

 SIGNET TRADEMARK REG. U.S. PAT. OFF. AND FOREIGN COUNTRIES
REGISTERED TRADEMARK—MARCA REGISTRADA
HECHO EN CHICAGO, U.S.A.

SIGNET, SIGNET CLASSICS, MENTOR, PLUME AND MERIDIAN BOOKS are published by The New American Library, Inc., 1301 Avenue of the Americas, New York, New York 10019.

FIRST PRINTING, MARCH, 1975

1 2 3 4 5 6 7 8 9

PRINTED IN THE UNITED STATES OF AMERICA

To my mother and father,
in loving memory

AUTHOR'S NOTE

The characters in this novel are fictional, and any resemblance to actual persons, living or dead, is purely coincidental. None has intentionally been given the name of a living person.

While this is basically a New York story, it is symbolic of conditions for girls and boys in trouble throughout most of the country. Over the years many of their lives touched mine as I covered the prisons for juveniles that exist, incredibly enough, in twentieth-century America.

I am grateful to the social workers, prison personnel, church leaders, judges, and lawyers involved in juvenile justice whom I have come to know as a working journalist and playwright, who shared their experiences with me.

G. S.

February 1974

chapter 1

FAMILY COURT OF THE STATE OF NEW YORK
COUNTY OF New York ....

NOTICE OF TRANSFER:

From: The Children's Shelter ....

To: Rip Van Winkle Center for Girls (state ......
training school) ....

In Re: SHELLEY CLARK, aged sixteen (PINS) ....

...who was remanded to us temporarily
by the Court is returned to Rip Van
Winkle Center, after latest escape from
your Center...being a Person in Need of
Supervision (PINS)....

Just a few hours before she ran again from the Center, Shelley looked dazzlingly new.

Showered and outwardly calm, she stood on the stoop of the hospital wing in the sunshine, her loose blonde hair brushed to a silk shine, her hazel eyes revealing nothing. She kept them averted from matron. She wore the white cotton overblouse, blue slacks, and sandals provided by the Rip Van Winkle Center for Girls, as the upstate training school was known. But the bright red corduroy safari jacket was her own. It was the last thing she'd bought before being hauled back again. With its shout of color, big pockets, and brass buttons, the jacket had said "Shelley" to her from the boutique's window.

Listen, it seemed to call out, this is me, Shelley. Different.

That was just a few days before they'd found her and returned her to the Center, this time in handcuffs and in ankle shackles. She had cursed them and struggled against being hauled back like some sort of animal.

"It makes life easier in the car if she's tied up," the transfer agent had told the driver, authorizing the handcuffs and shackles. "Can't have them worrying you."

"Them! Call yourself a woman, you bitch!" Shelley had screamed.

"See what I mean?" the agent had said. "She's already run twice from Rip Van Winkle."

They put her in the hospital isolation room, until staff made a decision on where to keep her. To the Center's girls, isolation was better known as the "stripped room"

10

because of its stark furnishings, high barred window, and no privileges.

Even during the week just spent in the stripped room, Shelley had been making plans to run again.

Run, Shelley, run!

Where to?

Does it matter?

Gotta go, that's all . . . been fucked up enough by all these goddam institutions!

Now Shelley stared into the sunshine. She took a moment, while matron waited, to savor the freedom from isolation. She tried to calculate how much time she had between this afternoon light and the coming dark, when she would run again.

Muted sounds of people drifted from the chapel area. People were talking, laughing, playing a radio. Of course. Sunday. Visiting day. She'd almost lost track of the days, in the stripped room.

She stared toward Cottage C. She wondered why people called it, and the other dozen rundown dormitory buildings with their thrift-shop decor, "cottages." More honest, she thought, to call the whole goddam institution by its proper name—a prison for young girls.

Each cottage, set near grassy walks or among the trees, and four hundred miles away from New York City, housed about twenty-five girls between the ages of twelve and eighteen. Some girls had committed the "crime" of being deserted by their parents, and the courts had nowhere to put them. Some girls were drug users and prostitutes. Many were runaways, or truants, or preferred sleeping around to sleeping at home. They were mostly PINS girls—known by that abbreviation for the legal term in their files: "Persons in Need of Supervision."

Mama was certainly not among the Sunday visitors . . .

No need to look.

You can't keep me here, you bastards!

You can't have me!

Keep running. Running . . .

Shelley bent down to pluck a dandelion. She stuck it in a buttonhole. She didn't expect the act to impress matron, who was accompanying her to Cottage C. Never mind. The gesture pleased herself. *She* mattered.

"That's sweet," said matron, mechanically.

She was an immense black woman, with three grown children of her own. From her on-the-job training, she remembered to applaud a positive act, like when the children plucked a flower. The professionals on staff, such as Jeffrey Olsen, social worker for the Cottage C girls, gave her a pain with their psychology and "on your honor" stuff. Matron knew it was she and the other cottage "parents" with their common sense who really knew what triggered crazy kids like this one: Safest way was, she felt, to keep 'em in solitary, lock 'em up and throw away the key, to show 'em you meant business. At staff meeting, she had strenuously opposed Shelley's transfer back to Cottage C.

She had pointed out that the transfer agent recommended the girl be placed in the Extension—the maximum-security prison for young adults a few miles from Rip Van Winkle, because Shelley had already run twice from this Center. "A more secure type of custody needed, because of her assaultive behavior" was what the notice accompanying her return urged on staff.

But Jeffrey Olsen ignored the notice. He was transferring her back to Cottage C. Shelley's old Cottage. He had arranged it, insisted on it.

"You'll be on your honor," he told Shelley quietly, ignoring the frozen look that he got from matron. Jeffrey Olsen believed in giving people another chance.

"It's not safe," matron had argued.

"Safe . . . what's safe? I don't believe in stripped rooms," Jeffrey Olsen had told matron toughly. *The tall, rangy, twenty-five-year-old social worker, only a year out*

her old companion on all these flights, knowing that this time, if she were caught, it would mean the Extension. Olsen or no Olsen.

Everyone knew about the Extension. Deedee's sister was there. She'd kill herself before they sent her to the Extension.

Shelley fought down the sickness. She looked at the figure lying silently beside her. Deedee was shivering with her own fear, but she was practical enough to have stuffed her tote bag with some fruit, Cokes, cigarettes, a couple of sandwiches, and a knife. Good for Deedee.

They lay there for hours. They watched two official cars speed through the gate, one with the local police and one driven by Jeffrey Olsen. He looked haggard and lonely. So they were missed already.

Shelley waited until Olsen drove slowly back into the Center and disappeared down the winding gravel road to the cottages. There she gave the signal for their dash through the gate.

The gate always stood open. That feature of the Rip Van Winkle Center for Girls was part of the Center's experimental approach: to make the girls responsible for their behavior. As a result, there were five or six escapes every month. Nearly always the kids were caught and returned; so why make it tough and put us hundreds of miles away from our homes in the first place? Shelley thought cynically as they ran through the gate. There's crazy people back there in Cottage C. Some girls are on pot—the joints are brought in. Some are sleeping with girls. All the older ones talk about is drugs and tricks and where "the action" is—on Eighth Avenue and in the Village. Even Deedee's been in a mental institution.

I don't want that scene any more.

I'm only sixteen. I'll wind up mental myself!

Jesus, don't let me get caught!

They ran single file, Shelley leading.

They skirted the dreaming village, with its small shop-

ping center and movie house and bolted shops and the
ivied motel, all whitewashed and timbered, the way tour-
ists like their landmarks. The whole area was Rip Van
Winkle this and Rip Van Winkle that, here upstate. All
Shelley knew about old Rip, before she had dropped out
of school, was that he fell asleep for twenty years, and
when he woke up, the world had changed and he couldn't
recognize it.

He sure wouldn't recognize that world of girls.

She ran crisscrossing through back streets, which she
knew from earlier escapes. She avoided the four-lane highway; patrol cars might be prowling there, should the girls
try to hitch a ride. Instead she hugged the dark and the
walls and hallways and woods—Deedee imitating everything Shelley did—and they put on speed until they
reached the next village, five miles away.

It was really more of a hamlet than a village, with an
all-night diner. Still high on excitement, but weary, Shelley slid onto a stool at the counter.

"Come on, Deedee. Coffee."

"Think we should?"

"Sure."

Deedee pushed her stool closer to Shelley and sat down
gratefully. The white-aproned black man behind the
counter studied the girls. He took his time in filling their
order. He'd heard on the radio that the police were hunt-
ing two more escapees from the institution. In fact he
thought he'd seen this blonde in the red jacket in here before. But he couldn't be sure, and anyway, he didn't want
to get involved. Silently, he put down two mugs of coffee
and took the money.

"Where you girls heading, this time of night?"

A heavyset man with untidy gray hair, piercing black
eyes, and stomach hanging over his belt put the question
to Shelley as he was paying his bill. His tone was bland.

"New York . . . City."

"Whatcha doing 'way up here?"

"Why?"

"Just curious."

"We've got relatives up here."

Deedee giggled. Shelley sent her a cold look, and Dee-dee left off.

"Well, I'm driving to Poughkeepsie. If that's any help to you," the man said. The blonde looked good to him—style, good figure, arrogance. Maybe a bit young.

Shelley hesitated. "Could be."

The black man moved uneasily, rattling dishes. "There's a motel, girls, just up the road. Get some rest till morning. I think you should . . ."

"Knock it off," the man said.

"No, we want to get to New York tonight," Shelley said, "but thanks. Thanks a lot."

"That's my truck outside. I'm taking vegetables in to the market."

"Okay, Deedee?"

"Okay with me, then."

The cabin of the truck was spacious enough for three. The man handed Shelley in first, so she'd be next to him. Shelley knew his type and hated it. But a lift away from the area was better than taking a chance on the dark, deserted highway.

At first they drove almost in silence. Deedee meekly followed Shelley's example of volunteering nothing. The man didn't mind. He drove fast and unerringly, knowing the road by heart, left hand on the wheel, right hand carelessly brushing the well-rounded thighs of the tight-lipped girl. Shelley twisted away.

The night seemed so lonely out there, where the trees marched down to the highway. She shivered with mixed feelings of fear and guilt. After all, she was responsible for Deedee. They roared into the night, the relentless headlights shaping their way.

A half-lit motel appeared near the woods. The man slowed the truck, brought it to a stop in front of the motel.

"Hey, this ain't Poughkeepsie!" Shelley cried.

"You know Poughkeepsie?"

"Sure I know it! It's a big city."

"We'll get there. Eventually. Come on."

"What for?"

"You . . . ," he said to Deedee, ". . . stay here, watch the truck. Okay?"

He grabbed Shelley and pulled her out on his side.

"They make great pizza here," he said.

"Lemme go!"

"You'll like their pizza."

"I read you, mister. I'm warning you . . ."

"Listen, don't warn me no warnings," the man said roughly. "You're the runaways. I heard it on the radio. You don't want me to turn you in, do you?"

He stuck his bulbous middle against her, and for a wild moment Shelley wondered if a well-placed kick could burst it. Then a spectacular clamor burst on the night itself, and the man spun around and yelled his disbelief.

Crates of potatoes and cabbages and melons and carrots and tomatoes were crashing out the back of his truck. Deedee had used her knife on the rope that lashed the crates to the truck. Now they made a great broken heap on the highway. Lights came up in the motel.

"You bitch!" the man yelled.

But by then the girls were racing together from the scene, at first up the highway, then dodging into the woods.

"That was real smart thinking, Deedee," Shelley panted. Deedee laughed her satisfaction as they ran.

"He'll call the cops, sure," Shelley said.

Here I go, running again. Oh, Mama, just say you're glad to see me . . . I'll be good, Mama!

She pulled Deedee down beside her. They shared a can of Coke, gulping deeply, holding hands in the dark, trying to be casual now about the man.

"Boy, that was close," said Deedee.

"Just another dirty old man," said Shelley. She felt a mixture of hatred and sadness. "I been there before. My stepfather."

"Yeah?"

"My mother wouldn't believe me."

"Her own daughter?"

" 'That's a sin,' she kept saying. 'You shouldn't say things like that. You'll get put away!' "

"He should be busted for that."

"Put away! Put away! That's all they know."

"So why you going back there, Shelley?"

"I dunno."

"My mother wants me. I just know!"

"Yeah . . . me, too. It's gonna be okay this time."

Make it okay, Mama!

They slept. They hid out in the woods until the first light shafted the treetops and they heard a bird. The woods showed dimly green and golden, with clumps of field flowers. No time for flowers, Shelley told herself, pulling Deedee to her feet. Cautiously, still feeling hunted, they worked their way back to the open road. Shelley let the first few cars go by.

"We'll wait for a woman driver," she said.

It was a long wait, but worth it. A young woman in fashionable sports clothes, driving a station wagon, seemed glad of their company. She was talkative: So boring driving alone through the night . . . going to pick up the children . . . with their grandparents in Brooklyn.

Shelley smiled agreeably now and then, as though listening, her own thoughts running on in a kind of fantasy: Mama's waiting up for me . . . bought you some chocolates, Mama, with soft centers. Kiss me, Mama. And that bastard, Calvin, your husband—what? Gone?

Gone.

"Brooklyn," she heard Deedee exclaim. "That's where I'm going!"

"I'll drop you off there, then."

"Man, that's perfect!"

"And I can take the subway," Shelley said, "to Manhattan."

The woman kept on about her kids, a little boy and girl, having holidays with gram and gramp before school began. I've got a brother and sister, Shelley reflected. But I've never seen them. They're in California, I think. Where Mama placed them years ago. Wonder where California is, in case . . . I guess it's pretty far.

The station wagon sped along the highway, taking the curves confidently.

In Cottage C, the police were still haranguing Jeffrey Olsen.

This was the sixth escape this month alone, wasn't it? The people in the village were pretty upset, pretty upset.

"All the others were caught, or sent back by their parents, weren't they?" Olsen said at last. He was weary of the cops. The girls of the cottage, subdued and unwilling to answer questions, had gone to chores or class. Olsen stood at the imitation fireplace, smoking and drinking black coffee and trying to stay awake.

He held, under his arm, a thick, manila, legal-size file: the file on Shelley Clark. It seemed to have a life of its own, the way the Petitions and Orders and Complaints and Letters and Problems and Warrants and Recommendations had fattened it up over the years.

"This Shelley Clark, in that file you got there, she's escaped from here twice before, right?"

"She's not . . . in that file. She's a girl. She lives."

"She lives all right. She knows how to run."

"Yes, she knows how to run."

"Why haven't you done something about her by now?"

"What do you suggest?"

"Maximum security . . . the Extension. They'd know what to do."

"And when she comes out of the Extension?"

"What d'ya mean?"

"They all *do* come out, you know."

"So?"

"So what if she's still running—at age seventeen, at eighteen, at nineteen?"

"That's your problem."

"No, dammit, it's *her* problem and it's ours—yours, mine, the community's!" Olsen threw the file on the table. The focus of all eyes, the file seemed to dominate the room of adults. "Look at it! She's been running *since she was ten*. Now she's sixteen, still running. Do you want to know what her crime is? It's being labeled PINS—a Person in Need of Supervision. That's a crime? Well, let me tell you how I feel about her running from here."

Olsen slid into a chair. He passed his hand over his eyes. He stared at the file on Shelley Clark and took his time before he told them what he thought: "If Shelley can make it on her own, why *should* we bring her back here?"

chapter 2

FAMILY COURT OF THE STATE OF NEW YORK
COUNTY OF New York . . . .

| **In the Matter of** | **Docket No.** S7352 . . . . . |
| Shelley Clark | PETITION |

...the moral and temporal interests of
said Shelley Clark, aged ten, brought
to this Court's attention for the first
time, require that the parent's (mother's) custody of the child be examined
for the following reasons....

⚜ ⚜

Until she was ten, Mama had held on to her. Tight. Shelley's baby brother and sister, Stevie and Maureen, had long been placed in foster homes. Not Shelley.

"Shelley's my firstborn, my 'blithe spirit,'" Mama told the Welfare investigator, who looked bemused. "I'll never give Shelley up!"

Mama had named her after the poet Percy Bysshe Shelley, to celebrate, it seemed, a high, proud moment in her own youth. Mama had represented her class in a poetry contest for best diction, delivering stanzas from "To a Skylark," which began,

> "Hail to thee, blithe spirit!
> Bird thou never wert . . . ."

Mama came in first, and she won a framed color print of birds flying free to some distant shore. Mama had treasured that picture all her life. Centered on the living room wall above the couch, it caught the eye at once.

Mama left school soon after, when her mother died, and she tried to keep house for her father. Once when Shelley asked about her grandfather, Mama said with wonder and bitterness, "He went off with a neighbor woman. Dead . . . I hope."

Shelley never knew her own father. She was, by the age of ten, left to play on the street after school, till Mama got home from work. Late at night very often, too. The cops and Welfare investigator reported that Mama was an alcoholic. They warned Mama, in front of Shelley,

23

to give up the bottle if she didn't want to give up Shelley. Mama had clung to Shelley. "You won't get her!" she shouted. "I'll die first!"

At ten, Shelley wanted desperately to do four things: to write a book, because she wasn't named for a great poet for nothing; to become a nurse; to grow a tree in the back yard of their house on West Eighty-Fourth Street; to wean Mama from the bottle. Of the four, the tree seemed the easiest to realize.

In the tough concrete of the back yard, there was a mound of lumpish earth. Something must have grown there once, Shelley reasoned. The soil was so crusted over with stones and dust that it crumbled when watered. Shelley planted anyway—a tiny plane tree that the science teacher bought her when she told him of her ambition.

"A plane tree can grow anywhere," he said, "even in that crazy concrete. Try it."

She tried. She softened the earth and mixed it with all-purpose soil enrichment from the dime store, and she put down the little tree. But it wouldn't take the nourishment. With the first heavy rain, the tree bowed down and died. She stood in the rain, feeling its helplessness, and her own.

She tried seeds after that. She followed the directions on the package, which bore a photograph of radiant, multicolored blossoms. She planted the seeds, one by one, an inch apart. She watered and watched over them. Nothing came up. Soon the stones and dust reclaimed the mound.

"Whaddya keep spending your money for that way?" Mama demanded. "Nothing can grow out there!"

But she regretted her harshness almost at once. "It's not your fault," she muttered.

When it came to the bottle, Mama could be very imaginative. Before the Welfare investigator came, she would hide her "medicine," as she liked to call the bottle:

behind the radiator under the sink; inside a loose corner of the mattress where she and Shelley slept; in the muck of the garbage can.

On days when Mama was "too sick" to go to work, Shelley truanted. She stayed away from school to be mother to Mama.

Mrs. Farber, the Jewish widow who lived down the street, would bring in some food—soup and meatballs and mashed potatoes with gravy. Shelley liked Mrs. Farber, who was gray-haired and chubby and neighborly. Shelley thanked her and told her not to worry. Mama sometimes "had the shakes" and she was used to that. She felt grownup and able to care for Mama.

Once, when Mama looked like she was having a fit, Mrs. Farber called the ambulance, and white-gowned men came and took her to Bellevue Hospital. She came out in a few days, but by then Shelley had been taken to a "home." She was to live with a foster family in Queens.

"It's only until your mother wants you home," the Welfare woman told Shelley. The woman was young, and carried an important-looking briefcase and seemed very sure of herself.

"Mama wants me home now," Shelley cried.

"Not now."

"What about my school, my friends?"

"Mrs. Andrews has a granddaughter your age. You'll make friends here."

"I won't!"

"Her name's Martha."

"You can't make me stay!"

The Welfare woman patted Shelley on the head and left.

Mrs. Andrews was stout and wore a fixed smile. She walked very slowly, in great pain—because of her arthritis, she explained with that fixed smile.

The living room was cluttered with bits and pieces of

furniture, and the linoleum smelled of ammonia cleanser.

"Martha will be home soon. Don't be afraid."

But Shelley was afraid. She didn't know what was happening to Mama. She didn't know how long they planned to keep her here. Mama wouldn't know where she was. She'd worry. Anyway, all she wanted was West Eighty-fourth and the kids on the block.

She took her cookie and milk to the bedroom that she and Martha were to share. She sat staring at Martha's dolls. One was a Raggedy Ann, and the other a revoltingly big plush thing with a blind stare.

"What're you doing with my dolls?" Martha demanded when she rushed in from school. She was a year older than Shelley, string-bean thin with untidy brown hair to her waist.

"I haven't touched your old dolls."

"Better not."

"And I'm not staying."

"Martha, you be good now! Shelley's living with us," Mrs. Andrews called out.

"Why?"

"My mama's been sick."

"Yeah. They're always sick."

"You had other kids here?"

"Sure. All the time. We get paid by the State."

"Well, I'm not staying."

"Grandma, she says she's cutting out," Martha called mockingly, as though she'd heard it before.

"Watch the TV, kids. I'm going next door awhile."

Shelley could hear Mrs. Andrews' agonizingly slow, dragging walk.

"This is her day for cards," Martha giggled. "C'mon. You don't wanna sit here all afternoon, stupid."

She followed Martha down the strange street to the corner candy store. Older boys and girls were clustered around the jukebox that was blasting a rock tune. Some were smoking and drinking Cokes. Shelley's spirit lifted for the first time that day, but she still felt outside the scene and hesitated.

Martha pushed her in and led the way to the back, where some kids were dancing. Rather, they were "fishing," in tight embraces rubbing against each other and shuffling around a bit.

A boy caught Martha and they moved together like the others, Martha announcing that "the new square is Shelley."

"Hey, Shelley, want me to turn you on, too?" A big boy in sweat shirt and jeans stamped out his butt. He took her arm possessively.

"Let go!"

"C'mon, I'll make you feel good."

That was the first time Shelley ran.

She ran blindly, not stopping until she'd put half a dozen blocks between her and Martha and friends. At a gas station she got directions to the bus stop. She prayed that her school identification card would get her a free place on the bus to New York.

"Know where you want to go, kid?" the driver asked.

She looked scared but determined. "To my mama. She lives on West Eighty-fourth Street."

He nodded his okay, and let her sit in the front seat. He gave her a stick of chewing gum. He had a good-natured face and grin, like her science teacher. But she felt tense.

What if Mama wasn't home?

What if she was still sick?

What about Welfare?

When she ran up the steps of home and heard the radio going, her tears were flowing as she burst into the room and Mama's arms. "I ran away, Mama!"

"Well, I guess you did."

"I just wanted to come home."

"They wouldn't tell me where they'd taken my baby," Mama groaned.

"It's okay, Mama."

"You just bet it's okay now!"

They went to a movie to celebrate.

Mama tried. She tried very hard to stay off the sauce. She got a job in a coat factory on Seventh Avenue. She was very clever with the needle, and the take-home pay wasn't bad. The Welfare woman came, of course, but she was so pleased with Mama's "rehabilitation," as she called it, that she made some notes and very quietly went away.

But Mama got lonely. She was still pretty, and a new cycle began with her. She brought men home from the factory.

Shelley, doing her homework on the kitchen table, could hear them drinking and laughing, "switching on" the kids called it, in the living room. Later the place stank of whisky and cigars. Sometimes Mama would get loud. Shelley liked to hear Mama laugh, but those loud evenings when they switched on, she would bend over her homework or just sit listening in terror. She would pray, then fantasize, that the man would disappear.

Once, during such a fantasy, she was startled to hear Mama exclaim in an ironic tone, "Hail to thee, blithe spirit!" Shelley went to the door then, and when she looked in, Mama was on the couch, staring up at the colored print. Her clothes were lifted up, and a man, half-undressed, was heaving on top of her.

Shelley closed the kitchen door quietly. Her head hurt, and pain stabbed her eyes. She went out the back way and walked down to Mrs. Farber's. "Can I stay here, please?" she asked. "Mama's going to be out tonight."

"Come in, Shelley. Of course. Cup of soup?"

After that Shelley took to staying out late on the street when Mama brought a man home. She feared those nights. Mostly she feared that the Welfare woman would find out she was on the street and "place" her somewhere again. In the morning she was too tired to go to school. Truanting got to be a habit.

By the time she was twelve, she was having headaches that would last all day. In the school lavatory, one morning, a kid told her to try her joint—marijuana—which would "cure" her headache. The two girls stood close together as Shelley lit up. She was a quick study and liked the sweetish smell. The headache did seem to go. She didn't go back to class, but slipped out of school with her new friend.

They spent the rest of that day window-shopping Broadway, and hanging around the rooming house on West Eighty-fourth where kids and men could buy and sell "grass." They giggled a lot together, Shelley feeling that she shared a dark secret. There had been lectures enough in school about drugs. She knew you could be busted for owning or smoking or selling pot.

The street began to have a fascination for her now. Nearly all the kids' mothers worked, and there were few fathers on the block. The kids Shelley ran with now were mostly key children—wearing their apartment-house keys strung around their necks, alongside their charms. They were a wild lot, preferring to meet in one another's homes to smoke pot, or just hanging around, to going to school.

Antonio was different. He was two years older than Shelley, a tall, handsome boy with lively black eyes in a swarthy face. He was the youngest of four brothers in the big Italian family up the street. His parents were polite to everyone but distant, and very strict with their sons. The mother went to mass every morning, and on Sundays the whole family marched to church in their well-pressed clothes. The street took a lot of pride in that family.

Tony and Shelley had been friends for two semesters.

They were in the advanced music-and-art class and sang in the choir. Once Tony came home with Shelley to poke at the neglected earth where the tree died. "It would be tough to grow anything in that kind of ground," he admitted.

Shelley felt safe beside Tony, and forgot her fears and headaches. She secretly believed he was romantic about her. She knew that she loved him. The other boys treated the girls they knew differently. Girls had to let them do nearly everything the boys wanted, to feel popular. Tony wasn't like that. He never came to their parties. But he liked walking Shelley to their block, and one day she invited him in the house for a Coke.

They were in the kitchen, and she felt warmly close to him there, because they were in her private world. But the boy became uneasy when he realized they were alone. He turned to go.

"We're alone here, Tony."

"That's why I'd better go, Shelley."

His hand dropped in a friendly way on her shoulder, and Shelley moved against him, wanting his warmth. Her eyes were wide with happiness. Tony, looking at her flushed face, smiled with amusement.

"You're just a little kid," he said softly.

A moment later Mama burst into the kitchen. She'd come home early and had already been drinking.

"You bastard!" she screamed at Tony, who stood rooted with amazement at her appearance. "You want to screw her right here?"

"Mama, you crazy?" Shelley said.

Tony stammered, "You shouldn't be saying things like that."

"Mama, he's my friend. We're in the choir."

"Some friend! Right here under my own roof!"

Tony ran out. After that he avoided Shelley. For a couple of months he stopped going to music-and-art. She wanted to tell him about Mama, that when Mama was drinking she said crazy things she didn't remember later. But she was embarrassed, too. In the school corridors or lunchroom, they passed each other in silence.

She spent more time with the street kids now. And the scene at home changed radically.

She and Mama fought a lot.

"Only God and six cops can help me!" Mama would scream, using her favorite expression of self-pity when desperate or frustrated.

"Go to hell!"

"I'll have you put away!"

"You're the one needs putting somewhere!"

"Don't you talk to me like that!"

"Where's the bottle, Mama?"

"You're only twelve! Where d'ya go when you're not in school?"

"Where did you hide it this time, Mama?"

"I can't work and be watching you, too, dammit."

"You worried about me, Mama?"

"Goddam youass!"

"You worried, Mama?"

"Sure, I worry. Goddammit, Shelley . . ."

"Who's switching you on tonight, Mama?"

"Where'd you learn to talk like that?"

"From experts."

"Only thing can solve this is God and six cops!"

"God, Mama?"

". . . and six cops!"

"It won't work, Mama!"

But it did work. It was to change Shelley's life forever.

She had been to school that day, having come to an important decision: She'd speak first if she saw Tony. To her surprise, he was waiting outside music-and-art, and he seemed on the verge of speaking to her.

Then one of the boys grabbed his arm. "Come on, Tony—no time for street tarts!"

Tony brushed him off angrily. But he'd gone anyway, without talking.

Street tart! The crack stung. That's what they called her mother!

That afternoon she cut school and went to a pot party, a "gig" as the kids called it. They played records, smoked grass, and felt loose and high.

The Welfare woman and two cops broke it up. Everyone was shoved into a paddy wagon and taken to the precinct station. Shelley spent the night in a detention cell with three other girls.

"My God, we're getting them at age twelve now!" the captain said in disgust.

Shelley refused the food they brought in, and cried all night. Next morning, when they took her to Family Court for a first appearance, with a law guardian appointed by the Court, Shelley's head throbbed violently. Mama was there, white-faced, mouth clenched in a line of determination. She didn't look at Shelley as they stood together before the judge.

"I'm sick, and she's been one time in a foster home and ran away, and I love her, but I can't manage her any more, please, Your Honor," she spilled out to the man in the black robe seated next to the American flag. "She's become . . ."

Mama looked at the Welfare woman.

"Incorrigible," prompted Welfare.

"Incorrigible," said Mama.

Shelley stared straight ahead. The headache brought on black spots before her eyes. She barely heard the proceedings.

Mama, let's go home.

Let's try to be better.

"You feel she needs supervision that you can't give her?"

"Yes, Judge."

"You want to commit this child?"

Mama gulped. "I feel she'll be better if she's off the street."

The judge riffled some papers and stared at Mama. "And what about the moral climate of your home, madam?" he said sternly.

That shook Mama up, and she looked scared.

But the judge looked at Welfare and shrugged. "However, we're here mainly to decide what's best for this child. She's certainly learning more on the street than in school," he said dryly. He rubber-stamped a paper. The law guardian, a slight, harried-looking young man, shrugged helplessly. Here was a client whose mother didn't want her, anyway.

Mama, let's go home.

Mama . . . what's committed?

"Mama," Shelley said, "I'm sorry. I'm truly sorry and it won't happen again. Let's go home."

"Be quiet, young lady!" the judge thundered. "You have nothing to say in this court."

"It's for your good, baby," said Mama.

"Let's go home."

"We can't. I've signed the paper."

"Well, unsign it!"

"Can't."

Mama, what've you done!

What's committed?

I'll run again, Mama! I'll run . . . !

You and your goddam God and six cops!

chapter 3

FAMILY COURT OF THE STATE OF NEW YORK

COUNTY OF New York

In the Matter of Shelley Clark **A Person Alleged to be in Need of Supervision, Respondent.**	**Docket No.** S7352 **PETITION (Person in Need of Supervision)**

The Respondent, hereinafter called a
Person in Need of Supervision (PINS),
in that she is a habitual truant, incorrigible, disobedient, and beyond the
lawful control of her mother....

Her first glimpse of Juvenile Center for Girls, just outside Manhattan, was of a high wall. Fifteen feet of gray brick that segregated the institution from the rest of the community.

As the transfer bus with its barred windows drove her and the other girls into the prison, she couldn't seem to take her eyes off the high, threatening wall all around. Sprayed on the outside were graffiti by neighborhood "artists" ("Fuck Marilyn," "The Roman Debs Are Shits"), and political graffiti ("Fight Poverty," and "Right On").

The dreary, two-story buildings held administrative offices, girls' dormitories and classrooms. There was a stretch of grass and empty brown patches where nothing grew. There was a small playing field and wooden benches. And there was the wall. And a stillness everywhere, as though BE QUIET was engraved on the stale air.

"You were brought here," the girls were told, to await "final placement" by the Court. The Court was studying "what's best for each of you." Maybe she wouldn't stay long. Most kids were blacks or Puerto Ricans from the city slums. Some were here on PINS petitions like her, committed by their parents. Some were being held on custody petitions—the Court to decide which parent could have the child. Some were awaiting trial for behavior that would have been adjudged criminal in an adult, like assault with a deadly weapon, or for robbery or narcotics violations.

To Shelley, everything in the place seemed faded or forgotten.

The buildings inside had broken plaster and broken pipes. The dorms were crowded. Prison-issue iron cots were pushed one against the other, allowing no privacy for the girls. The walls everywhere were painted institutional green. The common room did boast an upright piano and a record player. But they were locked. That was the cruncher: Everything, including doors and windows, seemed to be barred and locked. Juvenile Center?

No matter what they called it, it was prison.

Uniformed women patrolled the corridors and supervised the dorms. They wore iron rings on their belts from which dangled immense numbers of keys, which vibrated as the women walked.

The windows were high up, so the sunshine barely touching the bars was locked out, too.

In the crowded dorm, standing beside her bed and footlocker, Shelley felt frightened, deserted. How many of the others felt as she felt—trapped?

"We are your family now, and we don't want no trouble," the guard said routinely.

Family! Mama, what do you say to that?

"School's in the basement. I'll take you there," the guard said. She escorted Shelley and left.

The teacher was conducting several levels of math at the same time. One large white girl, who looked about sixteen, was at the blackboard struggling to add 3 to 12. The teacher, a bespectacled, middle-aged woman with fluffy white hair, was saying with a patient smile, "Try adding it one by one, Rita."

Shelley stared at the walls, which were scrawled over, telling of other kids who had been here: "Dimples . . . Mia and Carlos . . . Frenchie from Staten Island . . . Get Movin.'"

She stared at the big girl at the blackboard, and the little kid at a desk who was sucking her thumb. She wondered if the teacher could do anything about her headaches. Her head hurt so much.

Quietly, she went to a corner and threw up.

The girls and the teacher watched in silence. The teacher was a "civilian," not a uniformed member of the Correction Department. She knew it was Shelley's first day, perhaps her first time in prison. She sent Shelley up to bed. She cleaned the mess up herself.

(*"It is the responsibility of society to prevent, whenever possible, the child's separation from his/her home," the teacher ironically remembered from the special training program for her volunteer work here. "To meet this responsibility requires services which are not now available to the volume of children charged with delinquent behavior. . . . Some children fare better in a family boarding home. Other children cannot tolerate the personalized relationships expected in such a family home. The alternative should permit the tailoring of the degree of control over his/her life that seems necessary, without posing other risks."*)

There were fifteen girls in Shelley's dorm, ranging in age from ten to seventeen. A woman officer sat for certain hours at a desk just inside the door, with a telephone, her keys, and a ledger that listed each girl by name, age, arrival date, and offense. She had the job of supervising the girls and keeping order. This included keeping the lesbians, in particular, from assaulting the younger girls.

Shelley was at Juvenile Center for two months, while the judge was deciding where to place her. Waiting and wondering and fearful, she felt under daily attack. Her dorm was typical of the whole prison. The girls constantly talked about their homes, their "crimes," and drugs. This was what they knew best.

Brooklyn Nancy was a fourteen-year-old white girl, with a speech defect because of her harelip, who told them, "My father put me up for cursing at him. I threw knives at him, and at my sister and brother. I don't know why. I want to be home with them." Like Shelley, she was listed as a first offender.

There was Joanne, fifteen, from the Lower East Side, a vivacious black girl, with a high "natural" hairstyle. She had cut a woman near her home who tried to steal her money, and the woman had needed twenty stitches in her chest. Joanne was furious with her treatment by an officer in the mess hall: "She called us ugly bitches and tramps! She said, 'I don't give a damn about none of you bitches! You don't faze me one bit!' Just because the kids at our table were horsing around. She twisted my arm. Is that any way to treat a kid?"

Shelley felt close to Joanne, who said her mother had told the judge to commit her.

There was Maria, the twelve-year-old who sucked her thumb. She was a delicate girl, white, with braces on her teeth, who never spoke to anyone except in monosyllables.

"She's got a bad hangup," Joanne confided to Shelley. "Her mother was mental and killed the baby."

And there was Ruth, a short fifteen-year-old with curly red hair and blazing blue eyes. She was a compulsive talker: "What am I doing in prison? I'm here for running away from home. That's all! My father put me in. I run because I can't stand him. We don't get along. I ran away ten times. He doesn't believe me, that I run to my girl friends. How'd you like to have a father who keeps telling you, 'I wish you were dead?' "

The first time she heard Ruth, Shelley shook her head dumbly. Ruth kept on with her story, as if the telling would make her believe it at last.

Shelley told herself that Mama would never wish that about her.

The group that Shelley feared most was the lesbian group. They were in practically every dorm.

They wore mannish trousers and man-tailored shirts, but she learned that even more than those items, the shoes and socks were the real "signature" of the "butches." They all wore sneakers with thick soles, and heavy sweat socks. The lesbians would switch their identities back and forth —"boys" one day, "girls" the next; but the one thing that remained the same were the sneakers and socks. They had a mincing style of walking, like giving a signal: "I'm a boy."

The Center's lack of privacy was fine with them. Girls had to strip beside their cots for bed, or for the showers. Stepping in and out of their clothes, some in desperation wrapped towels around themselves. This hardly helped when a butch marked you for her own. There was Mac, a big, rawboned girl with piercing eyes and acne, who told Shelley the first night, "If you're lucky, you can be in my bed tonight."

Shelley shoved her away. "I'll kill you if you try to make me," she said. She was terrified, but she tried not to show it.

Like some others, she didn't know if she could keep away from Mac and not get hurt. Little Maria put up no resistance to Mac. She didn't seem to care what happened to her.

"I ain't never had sex with girls," Joanne burst out one day in class.

The teacher liked to have a ten-minute "coffee break" when the girls could talk up freely on any subject: "Just ventilate your feelings, get things off your chest," she would urge. The girls trusted her. Maria, with her vacant eyes, went on sucking her thumb as Joanne continued. "I ain't letting it happen to me here. Like one butch says, 'It's gonna be easier for you not to think about what you're missing if you go with a girl.' They give you a hard time, man. It's no good!"

"Can I ask you a question?" Ruth demanded in a hard tone. "Tell me, why do they have places like this? We come in here for doing one little thing, like running away from home, and when we go back out we do the same

thing again, only by then we know about worse things.
And we should be trusted." Her voice dropped its fury
and grew sad. "I'm fifteen, and I've been here sixty-five
days, and everything's locked up—the windows, the
rooms, even the bathrooms. They have a lock, too, so you
can't go in when you want. I'll probably come back—the
way I'm going now—a butch. Why do they have places
like this?"

There was a silence in the room.

Shelley waited, with the others, for the teacher's reply.
She liked this woman, who had shown compassion the
day she arrived. No one had ever heard her raise her
moice or swear at them, like some others. You felt she
wanted to help. Anyway, you had to trust someone. Yet
the teacher's reply, which came in a monotone as though
she couldn't trust her own feelings, was no reply at all.

"That's a good question," she said quietly, "and I don't
have the answer."

In the two months that Shelly lived at Juvenile Center, Mama never came. Wrote a letter and enclosed
three dollars:

> ". . . told you're getting proper care, and Welfare
> says maybe it's better that we don't see each other for
> a while. This judge is a clever man who understands
> these things. He thinks you should stay where you are
> to cool off, and learn something good, till he decides
> what's best for you. I think he must know because he's
> had lots of experience. I've got a boarder now, to help
> with the rent. Love."

Love!
Yeah, Mama, I'm learning.
Like now I know a few butches.
Know what butches do, Mama?
Mac's very strong.
No way I can keep her off me, Mama.
I've tried.

Yeah, learning . . . real good, Mama.
Who's the boarder?
Has she got our room?
Or is it a "she"?

chapter 4

FAMILY COURT OF THE STATE OF NEW YORK
COUNTY OF New York . . . .

<u>INTERIM ORDER OF THE COURT</u>

In the matter of Shelley Clark . . . .

> ...above—named Respondent, subject of
> former commitment for being ungovern-
> able, requires placement outside her
> home. Her mother still continually
> drunk....

CR   CR

"Your mother's too sick to take you home just now," Welfare said, when eventually she came to transfer Shelley. "As you know, the judge has given you probation in a foster family for six months. If you're a good girl . . ."

"I want to go home."

"Well, it's not possible just yet."

"What about California?" Shelley said, desperately, "I've got a sister and brother there."

"That family's already complete," Welfare said flatly, closing the matter.

"Then I'm going home."

"Now the judge said . . ."

"I don't give a shit what the judge said."

Welfare looked shocked. "Where'd you learn to speak like that?"

"Where I've been for two months. Where d'ya think, man?"

"Now, you listen, young lady, you're getting this new chance . . ."

"Why do you throw us in prisons?"

". . . to stay free."

"I'll run, wherever you put me."

"Shelley, you're not helping your case!"

"I'm not a case! I want to go home."

"I understand."

"Well . . . ?"

Welfare shrugged, struggling with frustration herself. They were on a bus, going to the Lower East Side, and Shelley's appearance worried her. The girl looked years

43

older than when she'd brought her to Juvenile Center. She'd lost weight, and her eyes seemed unnaturally huge in her drawn face, pale with fear. She wished she could take more time with girls like Shelley, but she still had several home visits to make, which meant another sixteen-hour day for her. PINS kids needed more personalized care, time, loving interest if they were to change. Not this transient interest, which was all she had time for.

"Mrs. Farber on our street'll have me if Mama can't," Shelley broke into her thoughts.

"She's been sick, too."

"Everyone's too sick for us," Shelley said.

The couple who lived in the Lower East Side flat seemed decent enough. Their own children were married and living in Jersey.

"We like our foster children," the mother said breezily. She was the same shape all the way down, a thick woman with a neat, thick topknot of hair and a beginning mustache. "Hate to see them leave us."

"Call me Auntie," she said, after Welfare had made notes and left.

Shelley shivered. She hated to look at the woman. "I can't."

"All the others did."

"Okay for them. Are there locks on the doors here?"

"What?"

"Locks? Do I need keys?"

"Only for the front door."

Shelley tried the door to her room. When it opened easily, she stood a moment savoring the action. She went in and closed the door, and put a chair against it.

She was kept indoors a lot—following the judge's directions, she was told. But Shelley, exhausted by the prison experience and Mama's rejection, didn't mind at first. She listened to the radio in her room and read books left by her predecessors—science fiction and poetry for ninth graders and, what really fascinated her, the human, truth-telling stories of the black author Langston Hughes.

She went to school in the neighborhood, but the strangeness and loneliness and longing to see Mama became overwhelming.

Gotta see you, Mama. Who you got in my place anyway? You need me, I just bet.

She tried writing it down at first. Start the book she'd always wanted to write. She printed CHAPTER ONE on a blank sheet of ruled paper. She thought she would write about a mother and daughter who were separated against their wishes. Then she thought of Tony and wondered would Tony be loyal to her if he found out she'd been in Juvenile Center. She felt he would understand, and she loved him. No one could blame her for what happened with Mac! Or would he?

Oh, God, why did they put butches in with ordinary kids?

She stared at the blank page. She couldn't get beyond her intruding thoughts.

At last, when the pain of wanting to go home was too much, she tried to phone Mama from a public booth near school.

"Service has been discontinued temporarily," a recorded voice announced.

That decided it. She simply started home. This time she walked.

West Eighty-fourth looked about the same, only more so. Windows were open to the summer air, and the radios and Spanish music floated out in a lovely cacophony. Kids were playing ball, jumping rope, or just holding up the wall near the open windows. Cats prowled around the messy garbage cans at the curb, and street smells assaulted the senses. But to Shelley, the street smelled beautiful.

The super let her in. Mama, he said, had been away. Shelley went around the apartment, opened windows and all the doors. She looked down at the bare little stony plot in the backyard. She straightened the picture of the birds flying free. Mama had learned that poem; she must get it from the library and learn it, too.

She went to the bedroom and threw herself on the bed which she and Mama shared. She drew the coverlet around her and over her head, feeling it brought her close again to Mama. She cried with joy. She felt safe.

I'll be good, Mama. We'll never fight again.

She slept for hours. When she awoke it was dark and rain came in the window. She got up, and closed the little apartment in again, and switched on a light. It was getting late, past eight o'clock. She was hungry and restless. Should she really stay, or play it safe and go ask Mrs. Farber down the street?

She didn't have to decide.

Mama suddenly stood in the doorway, and Shelley was stunned by her appearance at first. Mama's formerly streaky blonde hair was now ginger red and very bouffant, her pink trouser-suit tight fitting. She wore heavy green eye shadow and false eyelashes. But what really struck Shelley was how *young* Mama looked.

"Shelley, baby, where'd you come from?"

Mama didn't seem surprised or angry or anything.

"I thought you were sick because they said the phone was disconnected," Shelley stammered.

Someone was standing behind Mama, a wiry-looking man holding a cigar.

"We were saving money till we got back in town, and the phone company's taking its time," Mama said.

We?

"I ran away, Mama."

"What else?"

"Wanted to come home. Okay?"

The man was in the apartment now, tossing his jacket over a chair, looking Shelley over. He was shorter than Mama, thin, with practically no hair and a strange skinny

Adam's apple that bobbed up and down when he spoke. "Where'd you run from, girl?" he said.

"Shelley, I want you to meet"—Mama's voice seemed unnecessarily shrill—"your new father. Cal, this is Shelley. Ain't she pretty?"

"Where from, Shelley?" Cal asked.

"I thought I told you she was living with friends," Mama said hurriedly.

"Why didn't you tell me, Mama . . . about him?"

"Well, it was real sudden. Wasn't it, Cal?"

He roared with laughter. "You might call it that, after being the paying boarder—paying for this, paying for that!"

Shelley felt confused. Mama was giggling like some hysterical kid at the Center. She hated Mama to do that. She wanted to hurt her.

"I wasn't with friends," Shelley said. "She put me away. Committed me!"

"Well, that's all over now. Say hello to your father."

"Real pretty, aren't you? Come and kiss your dad."

"You're not my father!"

"Now, Shelley . . . ," Mama said nervously.

"Don't be like that," Cal said, "not to your paying boarder!" And he roared with laughter again at his joke. "Well then?"

But Shelley went to her mother and kissed her, saying, "I haven't eaten yet, Mama."

"Now kiss Cal," Mama said.

"Okay."

Shelley leaned over and kissed him on the cheek. He nodded and patted her behind, and Shelley swung away sharply.

Welfare came, and since both Mama and Cal were working and wanted Shelley home, the judge agreed with Welfare's recommendation that she could stay—though still on probation.

She slept in the living room, on the daybed. But she hated the arrangement.

Cal rose first in the morning, very early, to get to work. Sometimes, when he thought she was still sleeping, he would stand over her bed, and Shelley could feel his eyes boring into her. Once, when the cover fell off, he started to put it over her, feeling her belly and breast under her pajamas, and she shoved him away, with loathing. She didn't tell her mother about that time. She wanted to forget it, because she was on probation.

Probation meant, Go to school, report to the probation officer, stay out of trouble, don't mix with bad characters. Probation carried its own stigma: At school, she now had a "rep." She tried to avoid others with reps. Some PINS girls on probation were hustling: expert shoplifters already, or snatching handbags, or pushing drugs, or sleeping around. Everyone knew who they were. They expected Shelley to join their scene.

She stubbornly kept away.

She never wanted to see the inside of the Center again, or people like Mac.

In art-and-music, she took a place near Tony who seemed handsomer than ever. He didn't move away, but on the contrary seemed glad she was back, and she felt deliriously happy in those moments. He even walked her partway home once or twice, as though tacitly helping her to avoid the others.

"They're crazy to send kids to prisons," he told her once.

"My mother didn't know what it was like, Tony."

"Did I have anything to do with . . . what she did?"

"Oh, no."

"Well, you'll be okay now."

"Only . . . I'm scared."

"What of?"

"At home. I can't tell you."

"Won't it pass?"

"I hope so."

They were halfway up West Eighty-fourth Street, and he could glimpse his mother waiting on the stoop. She had warned him against Shelley, which wounded his pride, and he hadn't replied to her. Still he didn't want to make trouble for Shelley or himself.

"Gotta go now, Shelley."

"See you tomorrow, Tony."

Until she was nearly fourteen, Shelley stuck it out at home.

Mama and Cal quarreled all the time, but the meanness was fiercest after they'd been drinking. Mama no longer looked so young. She let her hair go, and hardly seemed to eat, and dreaded the time when Cal would leave her.

"I can't stand being lonely, baby," she told Shelley. So Shelley didn't tell her at first about her fears of the man. The Center had instilled toughness in her own spirit.

But she feared Mama's and Cal's quarrels in bed. She wished they could all move to a bigger apartment, where she'd have a room away from Cal's eyes and hands.

One morning, when he came at her again, thinking she was asleep, she ran to the kitchen and got a steak knife, and said quietly, "I'm going to kill you if you ever try that again."

He never said a word that time—just stared, then turned on his heel and left the apartment.

But she took to sleeping with the small knife under her pillow. She was afraid now—of Cal inside, and of the street outside.

Some kids had grandparents or relatives to talk to, or visit. She had no one.

If she had a father, she'd try to find him. (Would he be the father of Maureen and Stevie, too?) Evidently Mama didn't even know who he was.

She knew one thing: She couldn't stay home. She had to run from it, before it got her in trouble again.

So she ran. This time away from Mama. And from the man Mama had married.

chapter 5

VIOLATION OF ORDER OF DISPOSITION

In the matter of Shelley Clark . . . .

...under the Family Court Act of the
State of New York, having been filed in
this Court by the parents, alleging
that the Respondent, Shelley Clark,
fourteen, has left home and violated
her probation....

She stood at the crossroads of Greenwich Village—Sheridan Square—and felt an odd mixture of elation and fear. She was unused to the sounds and rhythms of this part of town. Traffic raced around her. People hurried along in the neon-lighted dusk, avoiding one another. People were standing in doorways, watching passersby like herself, without touching.

Nothing touched . . .

That was good, wasn't it?

Everyone and everything left alone?

She felt sensitive to that idea as she hurried along, trying to fit herself anonymously into the rhythm of the street.

I don't even know where to go, Mama.

Girls I knew in Juvenile Center said you can make out in the Village. Get lost there. I mean, no one can find you if you're careful.

I'm very scared, though.

I feel I'm going down this goddam street and I'm not even casting a shadow . . .

They said if you want to be a together-person, get to the Village, lie about your age, get work and live anonymously.

Nice word, anonymous . . . from all that dictionary work in the Center.

I'm runner number . . . what, Mama? They gave us some figures in the Center—four hundred ninety-nine thousand, nine hundred ninety-nine. Something like that. On the run, from home and prison.

Now me again . . . even five hundred thousand. Half a million of us.

Jeez!

My head's hurting again, Mama.

It's saying, Who are you, Shelley?

Listen, Mama!

This is ME, Shelley!

I had to run from that house, from Cal!

I'm fourteen, five-feet-one, hundred pounds.

Blonde hair, very clean, loose and flowing like a veil.

Hazel eyes, sad and sleepy just now.

Mind going like a ferris wheel.

Love bright, bright colors.

Love Tony . . .

Hate my stepfather . . .

A heavy set girl, who looked astonishingly like Mac, down to the giveaway sweat socks and sneakers, called out, "Hi, looking for some action, honey?"

Shelley walked faster. She passed a tall, good-looking boy and his miniskirted girl peering into a jewelry shop window. They were exclaiming over some heavy gold chains from which dangled Oriental pendants. They held hands and looked happy. Shelley felt suddenly warmed by them, the way they held hands. They didn't care if people saw they loved each other. Touching . . .

She'd never held Tony's hand. What was Tony doing this instant?

Where do I eat without money, Mama? Where can I crash tonight?

Dig . . . this church . . . music . . . She found herself outside a small, attractive, whitewashed church. Its clapboard entrance and broad stoop were out of character with the nearby high-rise buildings and smart shops. The entrance stood open. She could glimpse young people milling around in some sort of meeting room.

A rangy black boy with a short Afro was starting

up the stairs. He paused to ask Shelley pleasantly, "Want to come in? We're having a hot-dog party and dance."

"Well, I dunno . . ."

"It'll be okay."

"How d'ya know?"

"We're open to all young adults. Tonight we've got a bunch of out-of-town visitors. Want to come?"

"You . . . sure it's okay?"

"Very sure."

He ran in. Shelley followed slowly. Free eats, anyway . . .

The freedom extended easily beyond the food. She found herself mixing with the others, many of whom wore her style of sweater and blue jeans. White and black girls and boys from high schools and colleges. Student leaders, they'd come from cities as far away as Minneapolis and Pittsburgh and Poughkeepsie, the black boy told her. The church had invited them to learn at first hand what life was like in New York City, especially the Village, which was such a magnet. They were going on tour the next day to observe artists and theater people at work, and also to visit clinics for alcoholics and addicts, and the criminal courts.

And could I clue you in to that, Shelley thought cynically as she munched on a hot dog and accepted a bottle of Pepsi from the black boy.

She moved to the fringe of the crowd. She admired their rapport but was thankful for their anonymity and hers. More and more student leaders were arriving, their greetings and laughter and the jukebox music turning the scene into a festival. She edged to the doorway, ready to run if someone asked personal questions. Then, with a shock, she found herself at a strangely decorated wall.

It was plastered from ceiling to floor with notices and snapshots of boys and girls—like those milling around behind her, yet not like those relaxed kids at all. The wall had a strange life of its own.

With fascination, Shelley began to study it and read:

From her father in Washington, D.C. Where is the girl, Elizabeth, in these pictures?

If you have seen her, call us collect for details! Illness in the family makes it urgent to contact her. She is 16--5'5", 100 lbs., long blond hair, blue eyes. She has many interests: Yoga, Zen, Women's Lib, communes, music, art, theatre. She has read a lot.

PLEASE!

There were snaps of a lovely, wide-eyed girl in a sleeveless dress and in a bikini. Shelley read on:

MISSING

Mary D. Aged 15, 5'6", 105 lbs. Hair. brown, last wearing moxicoat with blue jeans. Left home February 24, 1971, with another girl, Ronda, age 17. Ronda is familiar with the Village. Please contact....

$50 REWARD

Jonathan, age 14, 115 lbs., 5'6". Hair brown; eyes blue; clothing, blue overcoat with green hood, black checked pants, yellow shirt. A happy, smiling boy. The above missing person was last seen at about 4 o'clock at K . . . high school bus stop. Any information please notify: Chief George L. Browne at K . . . .

Shelley stood rooted to the spot, reading. So here were the faces behind the statistics.

She wasn't alone. Flesh-and-blood girls like herself who'd run from home in New Jersey, upstate New York, Pennsylvania, Maryland, Washington . . . A thirteen-state alarm for little, sober-faced Diane, whose four older brothers "are searching for her." A four-state alarm for Dick, "who looks older than 14 . . . father deeply worried and ill." Jennie, a black girl, smiling and curly-haired whose mother "begged her to come home . . . love her and need her."

There were about two hundred notices and faces staring and supplicating on the wall.

But about half boasted large red stickers. Over each of these was inked: "RETURNED" and the date.

Red . . . for happy ending?

Not for Elizabeth, or Mary, or Jonathan, or Diane, or Dick, or Jennie . . .

Not me, Mama.

No red sticker for me, Mama.

Can't go home.

Hate my home.

Hate it . . .

"As you see, we've been able to help quite a few." It was the black youth who had invited her to the meeting. "Have you . . . ?" He paused. Then he went on in a firm tone, "Have you run away, too?"

"No."

"Sure? Because . . . you don't have to be afraid here." Shelley was now all the way to the door. He followed.

"You can stay here overnight."

"What for?"

"If you like, we can call your parents for you."

She stared him down, her prison toughness asserting itself. "Stop bugging me."

"I only thought . . ."

"You just turned me off."

The boy fell silent, waiting.

"I haven't run, and there's no one to call."

"Okay, then, come on back in."

"Shove it."

He kept his cool. He was one of a team who roamed the streets of the Village, trying to spot runaways, to get them some help or back home. He knew this type—frightened but belligerently refusing help. Anyway, he wasn't psychic, and maybe she wasn't a runaway.

"Take our card," he said calmly. "You never can tell."

He stuck a small card, with a drawing of the church and its phone number, in her coat pocket. She glared at him.

She ran down the steps, angry and confused and very frightened. When she turned around, he was standing on the top step, a rangy, thoughtful figure. Same manners as Tony, she thought. He was only trying to be helpful.

"I'm sorry," she called up. "Thanks."

The boy nodded, understanding.

She hurried away.

The moment's rapport brought Tony to mind. She thought of phoning him, telling him to meet her in the Village, maybe bring some money till she could get work and pay him back. But she recoiled from the fantasy. Couldn't involve Tony and get his mother on his back again.

But Jesus and Mary, where can I crash tonight?

She was still in the more fashionable part of the Village, with its bright boutiques and chic jewelry and flower shops, and outdoor art displays where sweet-smelling incense pots induced passersby to slow down and look.

She was on Fifth Avenue, tired but impressed by the historic great-arched entrance to Washington Square Park. Even in the dark, the park with its rambling walks and benches and spreading trees looked like a promising oasis.

A handful of youths still played ball. Their voices floated reed-like on the night air. The public signs on green stilts were good-natured:

WALK, RUN, PICNIC ON THE GRASS,
PLAY MUSICAL INSTRUMENTS, UNTIL 10 P.M.

She walked in the direction of the ball players and sank down on a bench. She needed time to sort out her feelings. She felt terribly unequal to the task. She couldn't stay here all night.

Where can I crash?

Just tonight, Mama.

Someplace . . . not that church, though . . .

"Lookin' for a place to crash?"

Shelley was shaken by the raucous voice and the invasion of her thoughts. She stared at the young woman who dropped on the bench beside her. She was well dressed, like someone out of a fashion magazine, in a low-cut blouse and suede trouser suit. She wore very pale makeup and purple, wraparound sunglasses that were stuck on top of her sleek, black hair.

She held a brown paper bag, from which she lazily lifted a container of coffee. Shelley remained silent, and she went on in the raucous tone, "Don't be afraid. I'm not a cop."

"No fooling," Shelley retorted. She got up to leave.

"Sitdown, sitdown," the woman drawled. "I'm just taking a load off my feet. Want some?"

She set the coffee container on the bench and pulled a Danish out of the bag.

"Thanks, I've eaten," said Shelley. She sat down again.

What's the matter with me? She's only being kind, like the boy. Knock it off . . .

"I like to come here sometimes, with a snack," the woman said. "It's relaxing, don't you think?"

"I dunno. I've never been here before."

"Been walking around?"

"Some."

"Looking for a place to crash?"

There . . . she'd said it again . . . taking it for granted, or like telepathy or something.

"Maybe."

The woman nodded, and drank her coffee.

Shelley stared tensely ahead at the boys, who were now packing it in. Soon there would be no one but her and this stranger. She shuddered, feeling the loneliness in her bones.

Beyond the trees she could make our a row of grand old houses, landmarks of the Village, with solid white fronts and white pillars. Inside their living rooms, she fantasied, were high, painted ceilings and red brick fireplaces and great shelves of books, and people . . . families and friends telling the news or stories to their children. Her senses warmed to the fantasy. The woman's voice and offer brought her back to reality.

"I know one or two places."

"I haven't any money."

"I guessed that."

"Well . . . ?"

"Well, what?"

"Will it matter? I mean, I could work, I can wait tables . . ."

"Sure, sure, lotsa people in the Village help one another. Just have to know how to get to them."

"That's . . . beautiful."

"Yep. What's your name?"

"Shelley."

"Shelley what?"

"Just . . . Shelley."

The woman laughed. Her laugh was harsh, like her voice, and touched with cynicism. Shelley turned away uneasily.

"Have to trust someone . . . Just Shelley," the woman said.

"Yeah, I know."

"How old are you?"

Shelley was ready for that one. "I'm seventeen," she lied.

Now it was the woman's turn to look uneasy. Her mood shifted. "What if I put you in the subway, got you back home?"

Shelley sprang up. "You are a cop!"

"I told ya I wasn't. Cool it."

"Then . . ."

"It's, well, you seem damn young . . ."

"Listen, it's just for tonight. Tomorrow I'll be okay. You dig?"

"Yeah, I dig." The woman's mood shifted again, and now, with deliberate speed, she said, "Oh, hell, come on."

She tossed the remains of her snack into the bushes behind them, stood up, and shook off some crumbs. Shelley took a deep breath.

Have to trust someone.

Otherwise you can get stoned out of your skull, trying to work things out by yourself.

And it is a woman.

And she seems to know a lot of people.

"What's your name?" It was Shelley's turn to ask.

"Everyone calls me Sister."

"Sister!"

"That's what they call me."

Who were "they?" Well, keep going. For now . . . She would soon know.

The woman, taking the dark side-streets, sensed the girl's uneasy mood. She kept up an ingratiating patter: This was the more groovy part of the area, this East

Village . . . warmhearted people here . . . not so well off
. . . sharing their pads . . . no questions . . . hustling for
one another, for money and food and, yeah, jobs . . .
Shelley would like . . . her own age . . . meet them soon,
but not tonight. Tonight, Sister was taking her to her own
pad.

They were on East Second, a dreary section that was
frightening to the newcomer. Many tenement buildings
and brownstones were boarded up, with white-painted
X's on the windows, clearly slated for demolition. They
seemed doomed, like the occasional man or woman passing by, whose face looked doomed from alcohol and
age. Shelley knew the look. It reminded her of Mama's.

She fell silent. But tired out with the whole day, she
followed the woman called Sister.

In fact, the building which Sister called home wasn't
so bad. She had a small third-floor apartment, neatly
furnished, with a blue upholstered couch, matching
drapes at the shuttered windows, a knotty pine table and
chairs, and a marble cocktail table with a pot of plastic
flowers. The small bedroom off the kitchen was filled
wall-to-wall with one item—a bed.

Sister busied herself making coffee. "Sleepy?"

"Yeah. No coffee for me, thanks."

"Wanna use the couch or the bed?" The voice remained casual.

Shelley's throat tightened with tension. "The couch
is fine."

"Okay," said Sister. "You'll find the sheets and blankets and stuff in there." She nodded toward the hall
closet.

Shelley's spirits rose. At least she wasn't lesbian. "I
don't know how to thank you enough," she burst out.

Sister smiled and came over, and kissed her lightly
on the cheek. "Trust Sister to find a way for a real
pretty chick like you," she joked.

For one moment, Shelley felt like running. But where . . . ? And why . . . ?

She shook off the feeling. But when she lay down at last on the couch, she could hear her heart beating.

chapter 6

FAMILY COURT OF THE STATE OF NEW YORK
COUNTY OF New York . . . .

<u>CERTIFICATE OF WARRANT OF ARREST</u>

ANY PEACE OFFICER IS COMMANDED FORTH-
WITH to arrest the Respondent, Shelley
Clark, and bring said person before
this Court...to be dealt with according to law...having run from home....

The trust seemed well placed. At first.

Days with Sister were remarkably free of tension. They slept late and ate meals any old time, and Sister seemed to spend the days and nights more away than at home. Shelley washed the dishes, kept the apartment tidy, watched television, and rarely left the place except to shop for food. Sister gave her grocery money. She told Shelley to wait on the job search.

"They're going to ask for working papers," she cautioned.

"I . . . don't have them."

"I know."

Shelley wondered about phoning Mama.

"You can forget that, too," Sister had advised. "After what you've told me about that bad movie, you're better off on your own."

Shelley agreed.

But the neighborhood was oppressive, and she was often afraid. On her few ventures from Sister's home, she encountered scruffy-looking men who lurched against buildings or tried to block her way. It was more frightening at night. Surprisingly, Sister was hardly ever home before three of four in the morning, and once or twice she came in as drunk as Mama. At least she always came in alone. No men.

On the fourth night, things changed radically. Sister brought another girl home.

The girl was older than Shelley. She had dead-looking eyes, a thin pale face, long and frizzy black hair, and no makeup on. She wore an expensive, soft, champagne-colored leather coat, with matching boots and handbag. As soon as she saw the couch, she stretched herself on it, in coat, boots, and bag and passed out.

"Shelley, this is Constance."

"Hi," said Shelley to the inert girl.

"No home, like you," Sister hurried on. "Found her wandering around the park. I told her she could stay here awhile."

"Okay. But . . ."

"Well, the thing is, I'll have to move you out now."

"Out?"

"Just a few doors down the street. It's like a commune."

"No, I don't think so."

"You'll see, you'll like it. They're my friends. And . . . I'm working on a job for you."

"Yeah? Where?"

"Well, it's late. Let's get you settled first."

The new girl was stirring, muttering.

"She'll be comin' round soon," Sister confided as she locked the door behind her, and she and Shelley went down. "Just needs another fix."

Shelley felt scared and uptight. "How do you know, Sister?"

"Good vibes, gotta have good vibes, that's all it takes," Sister said with her harsh laugh. Her remark seemed to break her up and she could hardly stop the laughter.

Vibes . . . vibrations . . .

That all?

How many girls you had vibes out for, Sister?

That girl was flipped out.

Split . . . or not? Come on, Shelley!

Before Shelley could make up her mind, they were entering one of the buildings marked for demolition. It seemed deserted. The fear churned through her again.

The stairs leading up were dangerously broken and filthy. There was no electric light anywhere. Roaches ran up the walls.

Sister paused before a door decorated with an abstract art poster in psychedelic colors. She rapped twice, then once again, like a signal. Shelley could hear a rustling inside.

"Open up, Cowpoke!"

"That you, Sister?"

"That's me!"

The door opened a crack. The youth peering out, finally opening the door, was heavily bearded. He had the vague eyes of an alcoholic or a junkie. He waved them in.

The scene shook Shelley up. It was a horror chamber. Dirty, torn mattresses filled the floor. Socks and underwear hung on a rope near the fire escape. Cigarette butts, torn newspapers, rags, plastic cups were strewn on the mattresses and in the sink, where bugs scurried and slid. The human sight was the worst. Several couples, white and mixed, were stretched out or sitting up on the mattresses. Some were sleeping. Others were using some dope: Through funnels made from bits of newspaper, they took turns sniffing the stuff, first up one nostril, then the other. Shelley recognized the symptoms and smells from prison.

The old hurt began in her head, began pounding her temples. She felt terrified and turned to go.

Run, Shelley, run.

Get back to the street.

Somehow.

Sister took the play away from her. "Just for tonight, Shelley. Tomorrow we'll shop around for a nice room and the job."

"Just tonight?"

"Sure. It's too late for anything else. Cowpoke'll take care of you. Okay, Cowpoke?"

Cowpoke was wide awake now.

"Sister, do I have to . . ."

"Yeah, you have to," Cowpoke put in slowly.

In the moment that Shelley turned toward him, Sister was gone. Shelley felt the fear paralyze her. This scene was worse than anything she'd experienced in or out of prison. These people were really spaced out.

Cowpoke locked the door and pocketed the key. "Get some air on the fire escape an' I'll psych them off that there area," he said to Shelley, nodding to one couple spread sideways near the bathroom.

Shelley nodded dumbly. Maybe there was a way down from the fire escape. She edged around mattresses and bodies, and got out to the fresh air. She stared down at the dreary street. It wasn't a real fire escape—just an iron balcony, leading nowhere. She stood there, her back to the now-silent room.

Trying to figure a way out of this mess. Ironically, she thought of Mama's chronic "solution" of "God and six cops." It would take God and six cops to help her now. Feign sickness, . . . something!

"Come on. All clear," Cowpoke called. He stretched out on the mattress he'd cleared. He looked confident, his hands back of his head.

"No way!" she screamed, and ran to the door.

Cowpoke came up behind her. "You can't go now, man," he said. "You know us. You've seen our pad."

"No, I've never seen it! Never been here! I'm sick. Lemme go! Please, Cowpoke, listen to me . . . !"

He smacked her then across her mouth. The blood started as her teeth cut her lower lip. When she screamed and fought against him and kicked him, he smacked her again and again. No one on the floor paid any heed. Finally, a boy called out, "Cool it, Cowpoke. You don't want the fuzz!"

Cowpoke dragged her over to the mattress. He threw her on it, stood a moment towering above her. She was terrified that he was going to step on her, smash her like a bug. He got down beside her and pulled her head back as he unzipped her blue jeans.

For days and nights after that she lived in the nightmare. Sister never came. Shelley remembered moments when she ate some pizza and drank coffee. The coffee was spiked, she figured later, because she could "hear" colors, and at one time she thought her feet were hanging up on the wall.

When, much later, she tried to assemble those hours, they fogged up; she couldn't force herself to remember just who was there, what they did, where they went . . . except Cowpoke, who never went anywhere. Sometimes someone got up and went out and came back with the pizza and Pepsis. Cowpoke would distribute the food and make coffee.

Once a well-groomed girl who looked like Constance, in her leather coat and boots, was brought in. Shelley thought she glimpsed Sister. Most of the time—how long? —she hardly shifted from her corner of the room. She felt ill, and only half-alive.

One night she awoke out of a deep sleep, and became aware of the strange silence in the room. As she struggled out of the last of her sleep, she realized that she was alone. Everyone was gone.

With a sob, she got to her feet. Her mouth felt desert-dry. Her clothes were as filthy as the mattresses. Her hair seemed sticky. She tried the door, and it now opened easily.

If only I could see myself, she thought.

Never mind.

Get out while you can.

It was not until she was in the street that she realized why the others had split. A police car stood at the curb. The girl who looked like Constance—it *was* Constance —was being helped in by a patrolman. Shelley recognized the black youth from the church, and in the instant he recognized her. He looked sad and confused.

"Constance managed to phone her mother in Scarsdale that she wanted to come home. She remembered being here," he explained. "Everyone else . . . split."

"That bastard Cowpoke?"

"Him, too, I guess. There's no one but you now."

"The woman they call Sister? Constance stayed with her."

"Skipped."

"Better come back upstairs with us now, miss," a cop said, and led the way himself.

He looked sick as he poked his billy in the garbage and along the mattresses. Gingerly he gathered some varicolored pills in an envelope. He put a padlock on the door and, downstairs, another on the entrance. He told Shelley she was under arrest. She was taken to the precinct station, fingerprinted, and booked.

The more she protested that she didn't know who the others were, except for Cowpoke and Sister, the more the captain grew silent. She was allowed one phone call.

She telephoned Mama. "Listen, Mama, please listen . . .!"

"Don't want to. Can't handle you."

"I've been ill, Mama. Let me come home!"

Mama only cried, and hung up.

The cops gave Shelley something nourishing to eat— hot soup, a hamburger, milk—but she couldn't keep it down, and she had no way to bathe or really clean herself before the arraignment in Family Court. When Mama saw her, she wouldn't touch Shelley.

"I could get a disease just looking at you!" she said with revulsion.

"Can I come, Mama? I'm sorry."

"You'll run again."

"No, never! I swear it!"

"Only God and six cops, Shelley . . . !"

"Mama, listen, please!"

"You'll get me in worse trouble."

"You?"

"Yeah. Cal's threatening to leave me."

"Oh, Mama, maybe . . . maybe if he . . ."

"Only God and six cops!"

"Jeez! You and your God and six cops! Why won't you ever listen?"

Nor would the judge listen. The cops' report on the East Second Street pad was "evidence enough," he said. He wrote something in her file, brought his rubber stamp down firmly on the page, and said he was placing her in the remand juvenile shelter again, outside Manhattan. That would be temporary, he said, prior to committing her to the state training school upstate.

"It's called the Rip Van Winkle Center for Girls—for Persons in Need of Supervision," he said. "See that you make something of yourself there. The opportunities for learning and growing up abound," he intoned.

This goddam judge is no different from Cowpoke. He's stepping on me, like Cowpoke, like I was a bug.

The judge also ordered arrest warrants issued for Cowpoke, operating a crash-pad "for the purpose of narcotics abuse," and for Sister, "loitering for the purpose of prostitution and procuring."

The file on Shelley Clark was fattening.

Shelley was returned to the remand shelter, until arrangements were completed for her transfer upstate to Rip Van Winkle. The probation officer assigned to check into her case history and deeds was new: a young black woman this time, nice-looking and polite but very remote.

All that really mattered was that Mama hadn't listened. Hadn't tried to intervene with the judge. Again. No one was listening . . .

At the remand shelter, the dormitory was on a different floor this time. But it was familiar enough.

Shelley sat quietly on the iron cot.

They're not going to keep me here, they said.

You're very stupid, Mama, know that? Cal's a bastard. Looking for an excuse to leave you. And you know what? Putting me away again like this, you think, makes you look good to him. But that makes you a bastard, too, Mama!

I guess I hate you more than him.

More than him even.

I asked about Mac.

Yeah, she's gone.

But there are other Macs here.

Plenty.

chapter 7

NOW, THEREFORE, WE COMMAND YOU...to
take the body of said Respondent, Shelley Clark, and safely keep her in close
custody in the Rip Van Winkle Center
for Girls, for a period not to exceed
eighteen months....

The thing that startled Shelley, the first time she saw Rip Van Winkle Center for Girls, was the main gate.

It stood open and unguarded.

The bus drive upstate to Rip Van Winkle by transfer bus from the New York City remand center hadn't been too unpleasant. None of the dozen girls, accompanied by a uniformed woman attendant, had much to say. Autumn sunshine lighted the bus, and midway the attendant broke out cheese sandwiches and soda pop. She sat next to a very young child, who cried all the way and wouldn't eat.

"They have kids your own age," she assured the child. "You'll go to school and take hikes."

The child pushed the woman away.

She can't be more than eleven, Shelley thought bitterly. She'll be murdered in that lot.

When the bus drove through the sleeping village, for which the Center was named, she let the serenity all around slake her anxieties. In her soul she still felt numb from her East Village and Family Court experiences. She'd had no one to talk them out with, unless you could call the probation officer's remote questions and psycho tests and charts talking it out. Something may have been revealed in all that to them, but not to her. All she felt, deep in her soul, was rejection.

Rejection and loneliness.

Numbly she watched the small private houses with neat gardens speed by . . . the trees with their leaves now

73

turning brown, red, purple, gold. She felt the old pang, remembering her forlorn effort to make a tree grow.

But it was the main gate—standing open and un-guarded—that held her. It was a great old handsome gate, with ornamental iron filings twisted into floral designs. It opened inward, drawn back against the high hedges.

The bus rolled into the parklike grounds of the "training school" and for half a mile drove the rambling, leafy way to the buildings. It came to a stop before a low-slung administration building and chapel.

In those last ten minutes, Shelley felt a growing excitement. All she had to find out, she reasoned, was the time of day or night that the gate stood open.

She was sure that the school had restraints. What prison didn't?

She was confused about this new kind of punishment that put her far away from home and the city. But on one point she was very clear: No one was putting her away, at age fourteen, for "a period not to exceed eighteen months." *No one.*

She moved passively through the processing steps. She looked straight and clean and pretty, and very passive. Staff seemed to get the message: no trouble.

The director was a quiet man, avuncular and stoop-shouldered. He gave the new group his usual briefing: Welcome . . . now, this isn't a prison . . . won't find bars on your windows here . . . open-type institution, which puts you on your honor . . . live in those cottages you saw coming onto the grounds . . . girls around your own age . . . classwork . . . privileges for good behavior . . . group therapy with your own social worker . . . we're here to help you grow up.

Grow up!

Among all these other human rejects!

How long, tell us, for Jesus's sake?

A month? A year? Longer?

More than a month and probably not a year, the director said in a firm tone: "Just as long as it takes you to show some change in attitude."

Cottage C, to which Shelley was assigned, had twenty-five girls, aged twelve to sixteen. The crybaby of the bus trip was here, also a couple of girls she knew from the remand center. And, Shelley discovered the first night, a runaway—Freda.

She was a sixteen-year-old Jewish girl, slender and sad-faced, with defiant brown eyes and a nervous tic in her bony face. She had known two days of freedom before being brought back from Brooklyn.

Each cottage had its own kitchen and mess hall. Meals were rolled in on iron carts from the main kitchen. Shelley chose a seat next to Freda.

"How long you been in, Freda?"

"Altogether? Thirteen months, so far."

"What d'ya mean, so far?"

"Eight months first time. Then they said I broke probation back home because I went with my boyfriend. He'd been in a training school, like me, for running away and petit larceny. Probation rules say you can't 'consort with criminals.' Dig that! Danny a criminal. He's even going to community college nights. My father doesn't like him, so the fink told my P.O. we were going together again."

"Oh, my God!"

Freda shot her a grim look. "So I got another eleven months on top of what I already served. The bastards!"

"That why you split?"

"I stuck it out again for five months, then I split. Now, I dunno how long I'm supposed . . ." A look of pure hatred shadowed her sad, bony face. "I had to split. I began to think I'd kill someone here, I was so fucked up."

"What did they get you on, the first time?"

"That's it, nothin', just this boy, I'm crazy about Danny, and he goes for me. But we'd have no place to meet except in friends' houses, where we could be together and, you know, smoke some grass. I'd stay out late some nights. And that upset my father. The funny thing is," she went on mirthlessly, "the bastard goes bowling an' stays out with all kinds of women, and the whole family knows it!"

"That's about the story of my life, too," Shelley said. "That gate we came through, Freda . . ."

"What about it?"

"What time they leave it open?"

"What time? Any time. All the time."

"You're putting me on."

The nervous tic worked in Freda's face. "Ain't you heard? We're on our honor. 'Course if you're caught, you cop another year or two on your old sentence."

"What are you two muttering about?" A large girl with a heavily freckled face and close-cropped hair leaned over from the next table. She wore one gold-plated earring.

"You know what the mother spook said to the baby spook, Billie-Jean?" Freda retorted.

Several girls at Shelley's table chimed in with the answer. "Spook when you're spooken to!"

It was the big current joke, and everyone burst into laughter.

"Watch out for that one," Freda warned Shelley later.

"She's not my type."

"Never mind. She runs the Racket."

"That what you call it here," Shelley said bitterly. It wasn't hard to recognize an older version of Mac.

"I just want to know in more detail how you managed it," Shelley said.

"What?"

"How you split."

The Racket consumed much of the talk of girls and staff. At least the girls acknowledged its existence openly. Staff—director, teachers, therapists, cottage "parents"—knew it existed and tried to shrug it off. It was discussed in staff meetings: . . . not pervasive, so why exaggerate . . . it's uncontrollable anyway in a community of disturbed adolescents . . . it's only "family" to a lot of girls . . . they need some kind of love . . . if the press gets hold of it, they'll exploit and distort the story.

So with the tacit acceptance of staff, it seemed, girls went with girls. The hand-holding, hugging, long, tongue-licking kisses, feeling each other up in showers and dances was open here. The "pecking order" in the chain of command was obvious, too, in group therapy meetings: Butches dominated the sessions.

Occasionally a staff therapist would try to get such sessions back on the rails. "I don't want to hurt you," one therapist told a butch, "don't want you to get angry, either. What I am saying is that life can be difficult for the lesbian. The lesbian has to look at all the implications of life. She's saying, basically, 'I want to be me, in the gay life, so boys can't hurt me,' But it's not all sugar and cream, and we have the responsibility to point out all the pitfalls so you can be aware of the problems. Also to those," he went on deliberately, "who stay close to you, and follow your example."

His speech that day made one or two girls brave it.

"Yeah, Jonesy's gonna be a faggot!"

"You're not goin' the right way yourself!"

"You can't get yourself together in a prison where you're locked up!"

"Boys, they make me sick! I can't have anyone tell me what to do. Either I rule or nobody rules." This from Billie-Jean, the large girl with one earring. That crack shut everybody up for the day.

In contrast to juvenile prison, there was little activity in the bedrooms, since most girls were locked in their cells

at night, and the cottage "parents" (two to a cottage)
more or less supervised the movements of girls indoors.
But there was a great deal of sex activity in the woods,
during free time and outdoor recreation. The weaker
and younger children were at the mercy of the stronger,
older girls.

Shelley and some others tried to stay clear of the
Racket. But being a loner was not only tough but also
made a girl conspicuous. A strange girl, with stringy
brown hair and watery eyes, told her meekly, "I'm in the
Racket 'cause you gotta have a friend. It's too lonely
here." She was called Deedee, and she'd been in a mental
institution, as had some others in Cottage C.

Shelley didn't want to stick too close to the "mentals,"
as they were called. Nor to Freda. The butches had
been goading Freda after she'd split and been caught.
They taunted her about her boyfriend, wanted to know
how many boys she really slept with.

"I ran," said Freda hotly, the nervous tic working
away, "because I'm not a criminal, and I wanted to be
free of all you goddam butches!"

Next day someone found Freda in the bathroom
with two blade cuts in her shoulder, bleeding badly. She
was rushed to the infirmary. No, she muttered, she didn't
know who did it. After that, Freda volunteered nothing
to anyone. She sat silent in group meetings. She avoided
the butches and went on long, lonely walks.

"She shoulda taken her own advice," Shelley told
herself.

She, too, was driven by a searing loneliness. She felt
she was a pariah. When she could, she got to the small
library on the grounds. Once she borrowed *Readings
in Literature,* and to her joy she found the whole of
Shelley's poem "To a Skylark." It was like finding a
friend. She read each line aloud, slowly and greedily.
She loved the word-painting in each of the twenty-one
stanzas, and for the moment didn't feel so alone. She

copied the poem into her notebook. She could see, in her mind's eye, the print in her mother's living room of the birds flying free.

She was shocked to note the dates of the poet's lifetime, under his facsimile signature: "Born August 4, 1792; died July 8, 1822." Then he lived only thirty years! He had been lonely, too, according to the biography. Dying in a shipwreck, far from his beloved England. Far away from home . . . She closed her notebook.

Cottage C had seven girls from Brooklyn, eight from Manhattan, five from Queens, and five from the Bronx. Although they were black girls and white, and some of Puerto Rican background, they could all have been sisters from the same deteriorating families and communities. Nearly all had a history of running away many times, or snorting drugs, or truanting, or sleeping around. Many had been committed by a father or a mother as "ungovernable." This came out at group therapy sessions:

"There's skin-popping in my family. My brother's a junkie, so I ran."

"I kept late hours, and went to my grandmother's house. I couldn't take it from my mother's boyfriend."

"We were all on grass in my family. Yeah, my sister's here, too. Cottage E."

"If I went home now, I might do worse. Like go back on the street with my sister. My brother's a pimp for the whole street."

And Marilyn, fifteen, a green-eyed beauty with fair hair and a cleft chin, told Jeffrey Olsen, the group's social worker, seductively, "I wanna be here instead of gettin' in fights with my father. And him kicking me out all the time. Guys wanna pick you up or rape you or somethin', you know. So I'd rather be here than messing up, with the cops on my back."

"Do you like it here?" asked Olsen.

"Yeah."

"Then, Marilyn, you've been here too long," Olsen said quietly.

Even the "mentals" understood what Olsen meant. The room fell silent.

Shelley understood only too well. Aching with loneliness, and fearing what butches in the Racket could do to "loners" like herself and Freda, she no longer resisted when Big Julia threw her arm around her one day and nibbled at her ear and said, "Don't get sore. I love you."

Big Julia was man-size and a hustler. She had three girls in her "stable" who ran her errands, and sneaked pot to her that visitors sneaked to them, and who cleaned up her room to earn her "love" and protection from others in the Racket.

It was better, Shelley felt, to have Big Julia on her side than to feel afraid all the time.

In the showers she let Big Julia understand that it was okay with her, then, when she let herself be swept into deep kisses as Julia pressed against her and ran her hand over her nipples. No girl or boy had ever touched her or embraced her so protectively. It didn't feel like love, but she felt a kind of sensual excitement, and less alone.

Who cared, anyway? she asked herself bitterly.

Well, maybe Jeffrey Olsen cared. He seemed to worry about the girls. And about the purpose of the goddam institution which closed them away from the real world outside.

Jeffrey Olsen tried hard to establish rapport with the girls of Cottage C. His motivation was personal.

A tall, spare, moustached man, Olsen took this job as social worker-therapist at Rip Van Winkle both to gain an understanding of himself and to work out feelings of guilt. It wasn't only his social-work orientation at Boston University that had made him decline a well-paid position with a publishing firm. His motivation was linked to a family tragedy.

His younger sister, Margo, had known a disastrous early marriage. When her husband deserted her soon after a baby came, she had gone from liquor to pot and pills. Everyone he knew in college was on pot, and he'd experimented with it himself. So he had closed his eyes to the destructive course Margo set for herself, until it was almost too late. She had just enough self-respect left to get herself into a private treatment center. Jeffrey and his wife, Nedda, now took care of baby Priscilla. He blamed himself for not recognizing his sister's need of him earlier, and the feeling of guilt was real to him. When the post of group worker in the girls' training center was offered, he was ready and eager to accept it.

The girl who interested him the most was Shelley Clark. Quiet, introverted, poised, too pretty, too cynical at an early age, rejecting attempts to reach her, she reminded him strongly of his sister. She never let herself go in the group meetings. She smiled indifferently when the butches took command. Gossip had it that she was in the Racket and "belonged" to Big Julia.

Instinctively, Olsen knew that she would run as soon as the opportunity was ripe.

He talked it over with Nedda.

Jeffrey had a high respect for his wife's judgment. And Nedda was sanity itself, Jeffrey felt, when she told him bluntly, "Let her run away if she has, to, Jeff. You couldn't stop her, if her mind's made up. And she'd never trust you again if you tried that. She'll come to you eventually, I think, if she learns to trust you. Meantime, if she's really planning to run . . . well, if it were me, I'd expect you to leave me alone."

He followed her advice.

He didn't do more than let Shelley know he was available if she wanted to talk. That he understood her desperation. That, above all, he knew and she knew she wasn't a criminal.

"None of you are criminals," he reminded his group-therapy girls one day. "You're PINS girls, and that means Persons in Need of Supervision *who got caught!* You were brought into court chiefly because your families or the judges"—he cleared his throat, trying to believe the judgment himself—"became worried about your behavior. They expect you to straighten out here and go home. Now, my door stands open to all of you, at all times, should you want to have a talk . . . about anything at all."

Shelley respected Jeffrey Olsen, and she liked him and trusted him. But she never turned to him for help.

chapter 8

<u>MEMORANDUM</u>

FROM: Cottage C Parents

TO: The Director

IN RE: Shelley Clark

...after initial period, during which she showed antisocial tendencies... Clark now adjusting, working without complaint, understands we seek a "co-operative family" here....

For three months, she made herself into a model prisoner. She attended classes, did chores in the cottage, went to chapel, went to group therapy, spent as much time as possible in the library, worked toward getting credits for "privileges." One such was the "dry run," letting a girl go home on weekend leave, but that came after spending at least six or eight months at the Center.

Another was an "honors" trip to the village, which could happen any time. That was what Shelley aimed for—it led out of the gate sooner.

What was the manner and time of running? During free time she listened, even while she read, to those who had run before. It wasn't easy. But the honor system of the open gate, with village visits as rewards for "responsible behavior," at least simplified the way. After three months, Shelley earned an honors trip.

Jeffrey Olsen told her that she and two other girls, who knew the village, had been selected to spend half a day on their own there, shopping for the cottage. Shelley felt dazed. She couldn't believe her luck. She wouldn't even have to run through the gate . . . she could walk away!

She kept her head, thanked Olsen without expression. He was, he said, offering her the shopping tour "on your honor, of course," and expected her back by four.

She took nothing with her that would arouse suspicion.

She dressed routinely—dungarees and denim overblouse and dark windbreaker (how she hated the dumb,

84

dark colors!). But on an impulse she tied a flowing red ribbon on her pony-tail.

She said no good-byes. Only Freda, looking up from her book of comics, gazed at Shelley a long time and said, "Stay loose!"

She had five dollars in her pocket and a list of goodies to be bought for the girls. When at last Shelley walked through the gate, she was confused by the ease with which she could *take* freedom.

Of course she understood the philosophy of the Center by now: You had to take responsibility for your own actions. This was a personal test, one of a series. If you were caught after running away, like Freda, you'd be punished with more time to serve. Most, nearly all, were caught and brought back.

Privileges taken away. Etcetera, etcetera. The girls knew it all by heart. And those who were determined to run said, at least in their minds, "Bullshit."

No one gave a damn about her, anyway.

No one knew she was even alive.

Mama never came, never wrote.

Yeah, she was responsible for her actions.

Including this one.

Her two companions on the trip had been at the institution over a year, and were expecting parole. They were boisterously happy. The shopkeepers knew them from previous trips, called them by name, filled their orders routinely. Shelley gave the girls the five dollars and her shopping list, begging off with the excuse that they were more experienced. She wouldn't want to be accused of stealing five dollars from Cottage C girls. She stayed quietly in the background while the others fussed over their choices.

As they neared the candy shop, she let the girls get far ahead of her, turned a corner, and slipped into the woods.

For almost an hour she ran, dodging through the trees,

avoiding the clearings, avoiding the highway which began to run parallel to the woods, hoping she was following the reverse direction of the bus which had brought her. She hardly paused for breath. She tried desperately to pace herself like a long-distance runner, to conserve her strength.

Never going back . . . never . . . !

Can't hitch.

They'll soon have a patrol out looking.

Find a bus going home.

Pay him later . . . somehow . . .

Or else hitch a ride later on.

Run, Shelley, run, run, run!

Sick of the goddam Racket.

Sick to death.

It was pitch-dark when she finally left the woods and decided to take a chance. She chose a neatly fenced, old-fashioned frame house with an ivied trellis at the entrance.

The woman who answered the bell was white-haired, with a gentle smile. She listened quietly to Shelley, then explained that the bus terminal was more than a mile away and hard to find in the dark. Perhaps her husband could drive Shelley there. No . . . no trouble . . . no, really . . . just wait a minute . . . he was going out on a late delivery anyway . . . sold plastics.

She turned back in the house. Shelley could hear some murmurings.

In a moment the husband, white-haired, too, but very straight-backed and all business, came out carrying a couple of small cartons. He gave Shelley a big "Hi, there!" as he got into his old Dodge and threw in the cartons. "Glad to oblige," he said amiably.

Shelley hesitated.

She was terribly tired.

Have to trust someone.

Jeff Olsen kept saying that.

She got in.

It was a short drive to the bus terminal. The local sheriff was waiting. The searchlight, revolving on top of his patrol car, seemed like a multicolored all-seeing eye.

"My wife phoned him. She had to. I'm sorry," the man said.

"You bastards," Shelley said sadly, to no one in particular. She got out, and allowed the sheriff to escort her to his patrol car, back to the Center.

The incident was reported to Family Court.

Mama didn't appear in court, Shelley learned later from her law guardian, but Mrs. Farber had gone with him. She had stood in the back, waiting, hoping the judge would call her as a character witness or something. But all the judge did was to announce, as he stamped some papers, that he was prolonging Shelley's "indeterminate period" in the training school. He indicated that she could now expect to do at least a year before any consideration of parole.

Another year at least in prison, for such a young girl, Mrs. Farber thought miserably. For what? What was Shelley's crime anyway? She couldn't puzzle it out.

Glumly, with a nod to the law guardian, who promised to let Shelley know she'd been in court to try to help, Mrs. Farber slipped out of the strange room with its high bench—but not before she read again the prominent legend in bronze above the judge's bench: "IN GOD WE TRUST."

Shelley waited nearly six months before she ran again. This time she planned her escape like an expert.

Several girls like the strange one, Deedee, had gone as far as the gate, lost their nerve, and come back. Staff began to complain that the gate should be shut, at least at night. The director, Olsen, and other therapists held out for continuation of the honor system. Their will prevailed.

Shelley managed dry runs of her own. Some days she went in the direction of the gate before, innocently, turning toward another cottage as though in search for someone. In fact she managed to explore the secret wooded areas of the institution. Once she buried two cans of fruit salad near a lilac bush; another time it was a bottle of Pepsi, packs of cigarettes, a dollar borrowed from Olsen ("just till my next allowance from Mama"—a lie, because Mama never sent anything), and a pocketknife.

She had grown thin and more withdrawn since her unsuccessful attempt to escape. She felt powerless, and resented the feeling deeply. She grew hard, and it showed in her eyes, and in her need to stare people down, and in the feeling she often had now of being out of contact. She had days of headaches and nausea, as though thrown back into the fogged-over scene on East Second with Sister and Cowpoke. It seemed incredible that so much could have happened in only fifteen years of life. When all she wanted—though she hated her—was Mama.

You had to have someone!

But she would never trust again.

Nobody gave a damn about kids in trouble.

Nobody.

Not Mama.

She never came.

She'd rather sleep with her fucking husband.

Jeffrey Olsen, holding back, was worried. It wasn't just the running away, and the harm that might come from hitching rides. He was worried about the change in Shelley.

With his director's permission, he decided to invite her to dinner with him and Nedda.

"Just have to try to reach her," Nedda agreed.

Shelley accepted, because she wanted Olsen to believe he could trust her.

The evening was not without its effects on her.

The apartment was warmly, casually furnished. It had an old upright piano, built-ins for books and records, a hi-fi and immense, comfortable floor cushions. Nedda served chicken-in-the-basket, which they ate with their fingers. It was baby Priscilla who took Shelley over.

"I have a baby sister somewhere," Shelley burst out as she played with Priscilla. The baby gurgled and scrambled all over Shelley, and the girl loved that. "Don't know exactly where. Some foster home . . . California."

Olsen looked at his wife and sent her a slight smile. It was the first time Shelley had volunteered anything personal.

"Want to know why I dig this evening?" Shelley went on, looking at Priscilla. "You're a family. Real. You listen to each other."

Olsen put on some records after dinner. While she played with Priscilla, and told her a story, Shelley felt some of the tension fall away.

"Maybe you'll come and baby-sit for us," Nedda said. "Priscilla's in love with you."

"Yeah, I know," Shelley said.

But she knew she would never come. She was planning to betray Olsen again, so she couldn't afford to let herself get fond of this family.

Soon after that, on a Sunday morning, she ran for the second time from the Rip Van Winkle Center.

She grabbed up her food-and-money-and-cigarette stash and the knife, and once in the village, she hid herself in a station wagon with a Connecticut license plate. When the driver stopped at a diner in Connecticut, she slipped out and hitched rides to New York City.

Only once did a man try to get out of line. When she pulled her knife on him, he stopped the car and made her get out. She walked until she hit a town, the name of which she never bothered to learn, and hitched more rides to Manhattan.

She phoned Mama from a public booth.

Mama let her come home.

Well . . . not really "home."

Wanted to see you, Shelley . . .

All Cal's fault she hadn't been up to the girls' Center. Cal said he was . . . was ashamed of her for having a kid in prison. Said Shelley was a tramp.

Okay, okay, Mama, but what do *you* . . . ?

So what I think is, Mama raced on, I'll have you stay with that nice Mrs. Farber, the Jewish lady. She likes you, and she can use a few dollars. The Center has already called twice to find out . . .

Sure, anything you say, Mama.

If they know you're properly taken care of, I don't seen why . . . Ohmigod, I hope I know what I'm doing!

You do, Mama! Don't send me back there!

Shelley let Mrs. Farber think she was home on parole. She hated to deceive the old lady, but the less Mrs. Farber really knew, the less trouble she'd be in with the cops if they came. And she didn't go to school. She didn't try to see kids on the block or Tony. At first she kept indoors. Once or twice Mama came to see her, and gave her money. That was when she bought her smashing bright red safari jacket with the big pockets and brass buttons.

Mama seemed frightened and didn't say much when she visited. Mostly that Mrs. Farber was a good friend, a good neighbor, and Shelley would have time to think what to do.

Mama seemed frightened and didn't say much when she visited. Mostly that Mrs. Farber was a good friend, a good neighbor, and Shelley would have time to think what to do.

"Shelley's good company," Mrs. Farber told Mama as she brought in a pot of tea and sponge cake. "Has a mind of her own, that's all. Why put people away for having minds of their own?"

So the old lady understood. Shelley sent her a grateful look. Mama's eyes were blank and her voice shook when she spoke. Shelley could smell the whisky on her breath at ten in the morning.

Once she went to a neighborhood movie, and she slipped in and out without attracting any notice. Once she was sure that Cal saw her talking on the stoop with Mama.

He didn't let on . . . at first.

Then came the day that still seemed unreal to Shelley. She had let herself into the old apartment, longing to move around the familiar things, to see her books, to stare at the print of the birds. The apartment was very silent. Mama was out that day, and Shelley had supposed that Cal was out, too.

She lay down on her mother's bed, as she used to years ago when they shared it, and lost herself in fantasy. That was when Cal had come in quietly. He acted crazy. He lay down next to her and tried to press himself on her.

"Lie still," he rasped, "not gonna hurt."

"I'll tell Mama!" she screamed, tearing at him.

"Who's gonna believe a tramp?"

She scratched his face and his ugly neck, and she left marks on them before she managed to free herself and run back to Mrs. Farber.

She and Mrs. Farber tried to tell Mama, but Mama turned away and wouldn't believe them. She pretended she couldn't see any scratches. Then she said Cal got them at work in the garage. She said Cal threatened to leave her if Shelley went around spreading lies about him.

Mama looked desperate and old, her looks gone.

Shelley never knew who telephoned Rip Van Winkle and told the officials where to find her. Mama wasn't around when the sheriff's patrol car from upstate pulled up before Mrs. Farber's house. A woman officer went up to get Shelley.

She fought the officer. She cursed the whole goddam, flipped-out, fucking system that was making her into a prisoner all her life. She called the woman a bitch. Mrs. Farber, white-faced and trembling, tried to argue with them: "Shelley's like my own daughter!" She wept, helplessly, standing on the top step of the stoop.

The worst humiliation was the crowd watching on the sidewalk. Mama wasn't there, but Tony was. He was holding his schoolbooks and seemed shocked by the uproar. He said something that Shelley didn't quite catch, something like "Take care . . ." before he moved off.

Take care! How? Where?

For the second time they brought her back to Rip Van Winkle Center for Girls, this time in handcuffs and leg irons. They threw her into solitary in the hospital wing . . . until Jeffrey Olsen came.

chapter 9

FAMILY COURT OF THE STATE OF NEW YORK
COUNTY OF New York . . . .

<u>CERTIFICATE OF WARRANT OF ARREST</u>

In the matter of Shelley Clark, **Respondent**

...transfer agent ordered handcuffs and
shackles be used owing to Respondent's
assaultive behavior, and foul and
threatening language....Returned to Rip
Van Winkle Center after second escape....

Olsen stood by her.

She knew he would. But could he persuade the others? It sook him a week before he got them to release her from solitary in the hospital wing of Rip Van Winkle, and to her old Cottage C.

She had learned one thing about herself in this last series of escapades: They could humiliate her and hurt her mentally and physically—the Cals and the Macs and Mama and judges and guards, the handcuffing and the shackling—but they couldn't break her. Something deep inside her they couldn't get to. She felt it, like some secret power. That was what she knew must be giving her the strength to try to run again. As she waited to be "sprung" from solitary by Olsen, and back to Cottage C, she was already counting the hours until she would run.

None of these goddam places was going to hold her. She would run . . .

Keep on running, again and again and again . . .

All through life?

No.

For their own fucking reasons, they treated you like a criminal if you ran, until you were eighteen. After eighteen, for some screwball reason of law, they stopped. You were "an adult," left alone. But until eighteen, they had the power to lock you away, just for wanting to be free of the adults who were hurting you.

Olsen had explained the law to them in their group sessions. The girls knew he was on their side.

Sorry, Olsen, I have to let you down again . . . The

grapevine reported, even before she got back to Cottage C after her second escape, how he'd told matron toughly that he didn't believe in solitary, and he was damned if he'd let them transfer her to the Extension and maximum security. Good old Olsen, whom she was already planning to betray again.

She knew enough, now that she was nearly sixteen, about being shoved from home and from prison to prison. She knew more about crime in all its nuances, and about children's cruelty and adults' cruelty in these "centers" than she'd learned in the outside world. People got worse, not better, in these places.

Anyway, she'd learned that was true about herself. The worst of it was, she knew she'd run back to Mama.

Still Mama . . .

Still needed to need Mama.

Need *me*, Mama.

Please.

Nowhere else to go.

I'm afraid of the Cowpokes and Sisters.

Gotta need . . . someone in life.

I'll keep away from Cal. Tell him!

Just take me back, Mama.

That was the third time she ran from Rip Van Winkle Center for Girls. The time she ran with Deedee.

Deedee had pleaded with her: Been here eighteen months, Shelley, let me split with you! I'll make it if I've got someone with me! And Shelley had said, Yes, come on then, it's too heavy hitching rides alone, anyway.

They had waited in the dark till the way seemed clear of Sunday visitors and officials, and they had escaped together through the gate, and went running and speeding through that Sunday night and Monday morning. Deedee, in fact, had been a big help when the truck driver had tried to force himself on her at the motel. They were lucky with the ride to New York afterward with the woman driver, and Shelley fantasied all the way that Mama would be waiting to welcome her back. She'd take her some chocolates with soft centers. Mama loved those.

If caught, Olsen or no Olsen, she and Deedee knew it would mean the Extension. Everyone knew about the Extension—the toughest training school in the state, a few miles from Rip Van Winkle. Deedee's sister was there: maximum security, with a high wall all around; cells with barred windows, locked all the time; time added onto the old sentence; no chance of escape.

Had to take a chance . . .

Last chance . . . ?

What else was there, if you were sixteen?

Had to be free!

They'd dragged her off before without Mama even knowing about it. You *wanted* me to stay with Mrs. Farber, didn't you, Mama? But they hauled me off before you came home!

Have to make up some story for Mama, though.

She'll never believe the Center's just let me go . . . after two escapes.

Get some story ready.

What did it matter, except she'd see Mama again, and Mama would protect her?

Mama needed her.

So she fantasied, with Deedee beside her in the woman's station wagon, which sped into the early morning hours, taking the curves so confidently.

chapter 10

FAMILY COURT OF THE STATE OF NEW YORK
COUNTY OF New York . . . .

CERTIFICATE OF WARRANT OF ARREST

ANY PEACE OFFICER IS COMMANDED FORTH-
WITH to arrest the Respondent, Shelley
Clark, having absconded for the third
time from the state training school
known as Rip Van Winkle Center for
Girls....

"Mama, it's me. I'm home!"

The apartment seemed terribly quiet, deserted, as though uneasy. Reflecting her own mood.

Shelley did not know how long she stood there, alone, clutching the Glad-Bag of chocolate soft centers that she'd bought with the dollar borrowed from Deedee. Uneasily she stared around at the familiar place.

Yes, the small palm in its wooden tub was at the window, trying to catch the sun. Table was laid for dinner, two coffee mugs upended to keep out the dust. The big framed picture above the sofa . . .

Blithe spirit! What happened to your blithe spirit, Mama?

God, let me stay. I'll be good, Mama, I won't tell you anything about anything. The room seemed to close itself around her protectively, not like the stripped room.

"Shelley, what're you doing here?"

Mama was standing in the doorway with a market bag of groceries. With her hair dyed red and frizzed up high like the young girls, she looked a mess. She seemed frightened by Shelley's presence, and brushed past her to the kitchen.

"You can't stay, you know."

"Mama, these are for you."

"Did you hear what I said?"

"Listen, Mama . . . it's gonna be different."

"They let you come out again . . . so soon?"

"Mama, I got nowhere else to go."

"I asked you . . ."

"Yeah, they said it's okay."

"I don't understand."

"They knew I didn't see you before they . . . they took me back."

"You're lying!"

"Mama, ain't you gonna say hello or anything? I've been up all night getting here!"

"You hitched in again? They wouldn't let you . . ."

"I had to see you, Mama! I can't stand it up there! Don't you understand?"

"So you ran again, didn't you? Answer me!"

"Look, sit down, will you? Listen to me."

"I'll get in trouble. Cal . . ."

"Mama, I've got it all doped out. I'll work, he'll never see me."

"You say that."

"You'll see, Mama, you and me . . ."

"And him . . ."

"Him?"

"He's my husband."

"Mama! Even after what you know?"

(Oh, God, I've gone and spilled it again. Get yourself, together, man!)

"You've been put away, Shelley, for telling lies like that! It's a sin!"

"Okay, Mama, okay, I'm sorry, forget it."

(I gotta stay here with you, Mama, make him let me. I'll say I was lying if you like, that he never got in bed with me and tried to rape me. I'll say I was jealous, whatever you like!)

"Cal says you can't come back here."

"Cal says! What do *you* say?"

"I dunno any more, Shelley. You're all grown up. You're sixteen, and you've got an answer for everything. You've . . . been around, you know. You can get him in trouble. Me, too."

"Yeah, I've been around. In every goddam foster home and institution there is. Mama, they took me back in handcuffs!"

"Well, they probably thought you needed control."

"Around my ankles, too.

"They . . . shouldn't do things like that."

"They'll never do it again!"

They stared at each other.

"Mama, you haven't kissed me."

She wanted to kiss Shelley and tell her she could stay. But she was too confused and frightened. Her married life hung by a thread. Cal had left her once. Her anger mounted.

"He says one woman in the house is enough."

"He says, he says . . . !"

"He's not been a bad father to you!"

(Not bad. Just rotten. How can you let him touch you, Mama? What're *your* hangups? So many dirty old men in this life.)

"Where's my real father, Mama?"

"I told ya!" Mama screamed, all her feelings of remorse and fear finding a focus at last. "You never had one! It was one of those . . . things!"

Things.

The word seemed to numb Shelley. She looked so young and vulnerable, the mother thought, probably the way she'd looked herself in those other days in her own father's house. She knew a stab of guilt.

"You can stay the night," she said.

"Thanks."

Uncertainly, Shelley thrust the bag of chocolates at her mother. She leaned over and kissed Mama on the cheek. Her lips came away wet.

She slipped out to phone Deedee from the corner grocer's. "I'm okay for tonight. You, Deedee?"

Deedee's voice, trying hard to contain her fear, told the story: "My mother's sick. She . . . she really is,

Shelley. She's had these heart attacks. She's afraid the cops'll bother her about me."

"What will you do?"

"I worked as a go-go girl once in the Village. I'm going there. They give you a room, back of the bar . . ." Her voice trailed off.

"The cops are in those places."

"Only you will know where I am, Shelley."

"Okay, then, where?"

"The New Image Bistro. It's in the West Village."

"Listen, Deedee, you okay?"

"I gotta find a place to live," Deedee wailed.

"Sure."

"Gotta make some money."

"Me, too."

"Shelley, you'll keep in touch, Shelley?"

" 'Course. Listen, if the cops come, I don't know where you are and you don't know where I am, okay?"

"Okay. That's our handshake."

"And, Deedee, look in your cigarette carton. I stuck in all but a dollar of that money you gave me. Figured you might need it."

"Gee, Shelley, you're okay."

"Gotta get back upstairs. Stay loose."

"You, too."

She helped with the salad as her mother prepared the pork chops for dinner. She put on the television and tried to keep her mind off the reformatory and Olsen and Cottage C and the warrant that would be out for her. Mama seemed too apprehensive anyway to talk much. She had a drink, then another out of the pint bottle of whisky that she kept on a high shelf.

How long you been on the sauce again, Mama? And hiding the bottle again. Who from?

The storm broke as soon as her stepfather walked in the door. Cal Williams, a small, wiry man, was a fast talker, a shouter. His Adam's apple stuck forward in his skinny throat, bobbing a counterpoint to his words. His grimy face, his fingernails, his faded shirt and levis held tokens of his work as garage helper. In the garage he averaged less than $100 a week and was fourth man—last to be hired, first to be fired when work was slow. But here, in his home, he knew the power of authority, which wiped out for him temporarily the day's humiliations and boredom. He used the power now.

"What's she doing back here?" And before anyone could answer: "I want you out. OUT!"

"Mama says . . ."

"OUT! Here's the door!"

"Cal, just for the night. I told her."

"And I'm telling her. OUT!"

"I won't go!" Shelley yelled. She didn't mean to yell. But he frightened her, with the Adam's apple bobbing away.

"Listen, Cal, she'll stay out of your way. They allowed her . . ."

"She's lying."

"Shelley, go in the bedroom while I talk to Cal."

Trembling, feeling her fear churn in her again, Shelley fled to the bedroom. She stood inside the door, staring at the hated bed where, not long ago, he had tried to press his body on hers. She had managed to throw him off, scratching at his revolting throat and leaving her mark on it. Now she listened to his self-righteous voice roaring over Mama's.

"She's trouble!"

"Just a night or two, till she gets a job."

"That piece of garbage in there nearly had them believing I tried to rape her!"

"I never believed her, Cal. I told you."

"She's already slept with every goddam boy on the street."

"It's not true!"

"No? Just ask her boyfriend, Tony."

"Tony's a good boy. He's from a good family."

"Oh, yeah. That's not what you told me."

"I can't turn her out."

"You done it before."

"That's . . . that's why I can't now."

She could picture them—Mama white-faced and trying to be whisky-brave under the verbal barrage, Cal trying to rationalize his crime. He probably feared that, someday, someone would believe her and not him.

The phone rang, imperiously silencing it all. Solving it at least for Cal.

"It's the Rip Van Winkle Center," he announced triumphantly from the phone. "They say she escaped with another girl. Escaped—you hear that! Ran away!"

"Cal, don't tell them . . ." Mama began.

"Yeah," Cal said into the phone, "she's here all right. I don't know about the other one."

There was a terrible pause. Then, "I wasn't going to . . . but, yeah, I'll hold her." He hung up.

Shelley stood motionless.

She looked wildly around the room.

She'd need a weapon.

Her mother's scissors, big and dangerous enough.

She caught them up, clutching the weapon as prominently now as she had, just a few hours before, clutched the bag of chocolates. She dashed from the room to the front door. Cal tried to stop her. But he backed off when she turned on him, brandishing the scissors.

"You creep! You filthy creep! Look what you married, Mama!" Shelley cried.

She threw the scissors at him, and they clattered to his feet, and she raced out to the street.

Running . . .

Where to?

Where this time?

Hail to thee, blithe spirit!

What the hell's "blithe" Mama?
Find Deedee!
New Image Bistro . . . the West Village . . .
Got no money . . .
Gotta help me, Deedee . . .
They're after us, Deedee . . .
Warrant's out. Cal will see to that.
Know what I feel, Mama?
Cheated.
By you and him . . .
Find Deedee, and stay clear of the fuzz.
Funny to be dependent on Deedee now.
Run, Shelley, run!

chapter 11

RIP VAN WINKLE CENTER FOR GIRLS

ADDENDUM TO CERTIFICATE OF

WARRANT OF ARREST

IN THE MATTER OF: Shelley Clark

DOCKET NO.   S7352

Stepfather of the Respondent, Shelley
Clark, reports that she ran from his
home subsequently, after threatening
assault with deadly weapon....

The marquee flaunted its name and style in neon lights: New Image Bistro—Topless Go-Go Girls.

Shelley stared at the marquee, hesitating. She was thankful that this was the West Village and nowhere near East Second to remind her of Sister and Cowpoke. But what was Deedee into, anyway? Shelley remembered the slogan that the girls of Cottage C had handprinted and hung in their recreation room: "Today Is the First Day of the Rest of Your Life." What life, Deedee?

She could hardly restrain a giggle at the thought of Deedee, with her slight and timid frame and wispy brown hair, a go-go girl. She studied the glossy blowup pictures which adorned the windows of the New Image—bosomy girls with bushy hair and nothing on.

She was completely unprepared for the scene inside.

A densely packed, smoke-filled bar with an iron foot-rail ran the length of the room. Men and youths, business-suited and hippie, crowded the bar. They were turned not to their drinks and bottles of beer on the counter, but to a tall, oblong, iron cage, standing on its own small stage near the bar. Just above eye level, it stood near a jukebox that was blasting out some rock music. The eerie thing, in the male-dominated room, was the over-whelming tension which reached up to the cage, where a girl was performing.

She was slender and very young and naked, except for the pasties on her nipples. Attached to the pasties were gold tassels, which she shook this way and that way as she gyrated. The dance was little more than a belly dance. In the small space she tried to fit movement to music, turning around, twisting low, shaking the tassels, standing astride and shaking them up while a hundred eyes followed every movement.

It was what the notice outside had promised—a sex performance—and yet it was naive, as though the girl, with shuttered eyes, didn't quite know what was expected of her. Once she almost fell. Her eyes popped open. Men's hands instinctively reached toward the bars of her cage, and she fell back in fear. Then, remembering her part, she drew herself up and smiled, her fixed, tremulous smile. And continued the gyrations.

My God, Deedee, you have got a body after all, Shelley thought. She stared over the heads of the men to her friend. The tears started quite suddenly. She brushed them away.

I'll never do that, Deedee. Never . . .

"You don't have to," Deedee told her later, as she dressed in a small flat behind the bar. She hung her crucifix on its thin chain on her neck. "I get paid twenty-five dollars a night three times a week, and alternate with another girl who does the other three nights. I told ya, I needed money in a hurry."

"So do I, but . . ."

"I'm never going back. No more institutions, Shelley. I got protection here."

"Protection?"

"You'll see. Listen, they need a barmaid. What d'ya say?"

"Just behind the bar?"

"You serve the drinks. That's all. Good pay, good tips."

"That's okay."

"We got college girls in the neighborhood doing barmaid work now."

"That all?"

Deedee grinned and hugged her. "I'll speak to Charlie tonight."

"Who's Charlie?"

"He runs the joint. Gave me this place to live temporarily. You need to crash?"

Shelley winced. She hated the word and its implications since East Second Street days, but she knew Deedee meant it differently. At least, she hoped so.

"You mean here?"

"There's plenty of room."

The flat was cramped but comfortable, with a couch and daybed, a lavatory, sink, and hotplate.

"You sleeping with Charlie, Deedee?"

Deedee's mouth twisted into the fixed smile. "Give you one guess."

"I guess yes."

"So?"

"So okay, long as he doesn't think we'd make an orgy."

Deedee laughed at Shelley's crack. Then, unexpectedly, she threw herself against Shelley's shoulder and held her tight until Shelley gasped. "What's wrong, Deedee?"

"I'm just so glad you're here, that's all."

It was late, and neither girl had eaten dinner. They went in search of food and quiet. In the Village, nothing was "late." The greengrocers' market stood open, with appetizing wares of cheeses and fruits and vegetables—great eggplants and oversize California oranges and ceiling-to-floor banana stalks. Arm in arm, they ogled the shops displaying exotic, potted flowers, costume jewelry from Mexico and Peru, and smart leather bags made by local artisans, and the bookshops still filled with browsing customers.

They decided on a clever little cafe near MacDougal Street. It had candlelit tables with gingham tablecloths. A black man in shirt sleeves was playing some gentle jazz at the grand piano. He was running lightly over the keys, trilling some old favorites. New Orleans-style, never looking up, playing seemingly, for himself—moving without a stop from "Birth of the Blues" to "April Showers" and "As Time Goes By." Shelley loved that theme from the film *Casablanca,* which she'd seen on television, and the loyalty of Bogart, and she felt a curious rapport with the strange black musician who played to please himself.

Shelley was famished. She was also embarrassed. "Can you stake me, Deedee, till payday?"

"Stake you! This one's on me. Celebration! You forgetting how you got me out of that goddam institution? Oh, Christ, remember that big fat slob with his truckload of vegetables!"

They rocked with laughter, remembering the incident and their narrow escape.

"Never going back, Deedee."

"I'll kill myself first."

They splurged—meatballs and spaghetti, green salad with blue-cheese dressing, coffee and chocolate sundaes. The Dixieland jazz rippled on. Shelley, hunger abated, warmed by the music and her friend's need of her, told why she'd run again from Mama.

Deedee never interrupted. She hung on Shelley's confidence. Their shared experiences and dangers, she felt, made them one. She felt closer to Shelley than to her own sister. They had come through so much hell together, and now they had each other.

Only once, when Shelley referred to her go-go act and she sensed a touch of cynicism in her friend's voice, did the shutters come down over her eyes. She felt frightened, fearful of losing her friend. Shelley had to understand.

"It's not forever. It's just a job, because, well, I have no skills and it's what Charlie wants me to do," she said. "Brings in the customers . . . there's another girl doing the act the rest of the week."

"You had a little problem tonight."

"But no one's allowed to touch us," Deedee put in swiftly.

"It's okay. I dig."

"Okay, then. You had to understand."

The piano player was leaving. The girls walked back to the flat together, arm in arm, feeling close, feeling like sisters.

Next day, Charlie looked Shelley over. She'd do, he said, thirty dollars a week and tips . . . tips were really good weekends, he said with a knowing wink. Lots of bigshots from the suburbs came in looking for some action . . .

"Not interested," Shelley said. "I've got to catch up with my schoolwork, maybe . . . maybe college later."

"You kiddin'? With that figure!"

"You better believe it."

"He believes it," Deedee said hurriedly.

Shelley learned quickly, behind the bar. Most of the men ordered beer, anyway; the others wanted chiefly Scotch, or cocktails that were easy to mix. The early evening hours were slow, and she could read then or listen to the radio. She borrowed books from the public library, poetry and short stories and American history. She hoped to follow through on the classroom work at the institution until it was safe to register for formal schooling again.

The regulars came in around ten thirty, the first show beginning at eleven. Then it got heavy at the bar until around two in the morning. She soon came to know the regulars—"You can call me Goldie," she said when they asked her name, and they liked that, so it stuck. She also learned to twist nimbly away from the moist palms of one or two problem drinkers.

It was true: No one tried to reach inside the bars to Deedee or the other girl. Everyone knew Charlie wouldn't stand for that. He ran "a respectable topless."

The other performer, a big-bosomed redhead with heavy thighs, left with a different date practically every night. Charlie got a percentage from what the johns paid her. Deedee would wait in the flat behind the bar for Charlie after her act. Shelley knew how to be discreet about her own comings and goings when the boss was with Deedee. Charlie had a wife and three kids somewhere in Brooklyn, and he never stayed with Deedee overnight. Only one thing could make him mad, said the nervous, balding little man with long sideburns and watchful gray eyes. That was if Deedee ever doublecrossed him with anyone else "on my property."

"No way," Deedee assured him, and meant it.

The girls settled into their routine.

They kept to themselves, fearing the long arm of the law. They swept and cleaned the bar and their small flat, which they got free. The pay and tips seemed too good to be true. They saved their money, and never went out alone. Shelley bought herself some new jeans, an Indian silk shirt, and ankle boots. Deedee treated herself to a sharp suede jacket with leather piping. Once Deedee put three ten-dollar bills in an envelope addressed to her mother. She was very proud of that, and very careful not to give a return address on the envelope.

"She's been real sick. She'll know who sent it," Deedee said. "It's better if she can tell the cops she doesn't know where I am."

In a couple of months they'd saved seventy dollars between them. They planned to spend ten of it on a Sunday boat trip to Bear Mountain.

The day before their boat trip, while Deedee was going through her act in the cage, Shelley found herself about to serve beer to Cal.

He'd come in for the show with another man, all cleaned up and slicked up, from his wide, striped tie to his best shoes. He was crowding forward for a better view of Deedee, and hardly turned to the bar to give his order. Shelley had the bottle on the counter and was twisting off the cap when he reached for it and came face-to-face with her. He knocked the bottle over and grabbed her wrist.

"You little bitch! You been up there, too!" The slightly stupid expression in his eyes told of some growing, inner excitement.

"Lemme go, you bastard!" Shelley stammered. She struggled to get out of his grasp. She looked wildly around for Charlie.

Deedee, doing her act, with the jukebox blasting away, drowning out all other sounds in the bar, was unaware of the drama at the counter. The crowd ignored it, except for few looks of irritation.

With the counter between them, Cal managed to shove Shelley down the length of it toward the door. Charlie was there, barring the way. Worried.

"What's eating you, man?"

"You got trouble, man. Cops are looking for her."

"What's she done?"

"Nothin'!" Shelley yelled. "Charlie, help me! This bastard wanted to rape me and I wouldn't let him."

Cal's free hand came down hard against her head. "She's gone to jail for spreading lies like that. She's my stepdaughter, and . . . and her mother's worried sick."

"What's goin' on down there!"

"Cool it, man!"

"What's up, Goldie?"

"Goldie, is it?" Cal spat out.

Shelley turned desperately toward Charlie, but Charlie was backing off.

Business was good. No one bothered him. He got his cut from the girl's johns regular as clockwork. Charlie quivered like a jellyfish at the smell of trouble. "Didn't know you been busted," he muttered, backing away.

"I didn't do anything, Charlie, listen to me!" Shelley cried.

"Whyn't you let her go? You ain't seen her," Charlie

muttered, putting up a front for some who were ▮▮▮ ing more excitement at the door than in the cage.

"The cops are on her mother's back. She asked me to take care of this," Cal said.

"You're a liar! You don't give a shit about me or my mother!" Shelley yelled.

"Hey, Goldie, he really your stepfather?"

"Whyn't you call a cop, Goldie?"

Cal wrestled her through the door and into the street. The street was deserted. He backed her up against the wall. Her head, where he'd hit her, was like a ball of fire. The terror which spread through her seemed to paralyze her.

He pressed himself against her, at will now, almost contemptuously. "That girl up there, all naked . . . she the one you ran with?" he muttered.

She struggled and tried to throw him off, but the struggle only served to excite him more.

A squad car was rounding the corner. Cal saw it coming. He left off, and drew back and straightened his tie. He grabbed her wrist again.

"God and six cops!" Shelley told herself bitterly. "For once Mama's right!"

He dragged her to the curb. "We been looking everywhere for her," he told the patrolman who got out to investigate. "She's split from the state training school. She's been dancing naked in there!"

"He's lying," Shelley said. "He's not my father. He's breaking my wrist."

"Let her go," the cop said coldly. He put them both in the back seat of the squad car, and he and his partner drove in silence to the precinct station.

She felt all hope drain from her. She knew her name and Deedee's would be easy to spot on the WANTED list. The warrants had certainly been out for both of them. Because of Cal, the cops would go back for Deedee, too.

had already told her about the commo_____ ___ would try to save herself.

Run.

Run, Deedee.

Run, my friend, my sister.

Take the money . . .

Get safe somewhere.

The cops wrote down some details from Cal. They told him he could go.

"So long . . . Goldie," Cal said. "Something you want me to tell your mother?"

Shelley, walking into the detention pen, noted his moment of triumph without emotion. She paused.

"Yeah," she said quietly. "Tell Mama . . . hooray."

chapter 12

RIP VAN WINKLE CENTER FOR GIRLS

NOTICE OF TRANSFER

TO: Director of The Extension Center for Girls
FROM: Director of R.I.P.
IN THE MATTER OF: Shelley Clark

> ...and Clark has considerable diffi-
> culty relating to staff and peers....re-
> sentful of authority figures...passive-
> aggressive, feelings of rejection...
> Psychiatric tests show she needs indi-
> vidual attention...has the feeling that
> people are not listening to her....

As Shelley expected, she wasn't going to serve the new time, added to the old sentence, at Rip Van Winkle.

"Three strikes and out," matron told her with cold satisfaction when she was brought back to the Center's hospital-isolation wing. She was to stay at the Center again just long enough for the paperwork to be done arranging her transfer to maximum security—the Extension.

Indeed, Shelley came and went with such dispatch that Jeffrey Olsen got little chance to oppose the move, despite the psychiatric test results with which he'd armed himself. Officials and staff were under attack, he was reminded by the director, for being "too permissive" with these girls. A couple of recent escapees had broken into a radio shop in the village and robbed it of money and pocket portables. He, too, believed in giving the girls, including escapees, another chance. But this girl? She'd used up her chances, he said.

Shelley caught a glimpse of Olsen as he grimly argued and waved some papers. He seemed tired and angry. He came over later to give her the news himself. A majority of staff felt she needed "a more secure facility."

"They're trying to kill me, you know," she said.

"I won't give up," he told her. "You won't be forgotten."

"Wanna bet?" she said bitterly.

The Extension was better known to its inmates by its nickname, "Hard-Rock Hotel." Running from there was impossible. No one got out of Hard-Rock Hotel except

116

after time served; if you were considered a real problem, that could take years. Even in adult maximum-security prisons, inmates could be considered for parole before the whole of time served. But at the Extension, release powers were in the hands of the director. He decided. And few girls were considered ready for the community until at least eighteen months had been done.

This was the real thing: High wall surrounding the prison, complete with iron gates. Locked. Long institutional corridors, bricked in, with barred windows. Individual "rooms"—in reality, eight-by-ten-foot cells with cinderblock walls, starkly furnished with cot, bureau, writing table, and chair; security mesh at the window; peephole in the door; door locked at all times when girls were inside their rooms.

And, for the most troublesome cases, solitary confinement. In a wing separated from the rest of the prison, solitary here went by the euphemism of "the quiet room." The girls laughed derisively at the phony term. And feared it.

Shelley moved through the processing as though in a dream. Her life had been turned upside-down again. She was touching bottom . . .

Who would listen here?

In one way, the Extension was better than Rip Van Winkle. There were fewer girls here—about sixty adolescents, deemed too unstable or uncontrollable in the relative open setting of Rip Van Winkle. Nearly half the girls were from New York City; the rest were from all over the state. With fewer girls, there were fewer chances for the butches to "score" or bully the smaller kids. It was also assumed that therapists and teachers would give individualized attention to those needing it.

In most ways, it was worse than Rip Van Winkle. Especially in the loss of self-respect and dignity. Shelley saw, early on, that because of the close confinement and watchfulness, the constant lockups and "headcounts," the girls were completely sealed away from the real world outside. There was a system of rewards and punishments— known, again euphemistically, as "merits" and "demerits." Theoretically, the system was expected to help girls "grow up."

One girl had stolen a cigarette from a teacher's bag at lunch; as a demerit, she was initially sent to her room and locked in for the rest of the day. She wrecked everything in her room in revenge. For such "uncontrollable behavior," the report on her later showed, she was transferred to a "quiet room," not without yelling and struggling against solitary all the way.

When Shelley arrived at the Extension, the girl had just completed four days there and was being permitted back to her floor.

It was at Hard-Rock Hotel that Shelley got the news about Deedee.

Deedee's sister, Christine, had earned several days' demerits for spitting on a house parent. She was a complete contrast to Deedee, a chunky girl with black hair teased into a bushy Afro, as vivacious and volatile as Deedee was submissive. During one "3:30," or free period, when most girls' doors were not locked, Christine slipped into Shelley's room. Her usual exuberance was gone. Her eyes were red-ringed and mad with rage.

"Deedee's dead."

"Dead?"

"She's dead. Killed herself."

"Oh, my God."

"I can't believe it!"

"But . . . how, why?"

"She took a lot of pills with a lot of vodka."

"You mean, it was an accident?"

"No accident."

"Oh, God. No!"

"She wrote . . . she would never let them bring her back."

"How'd you hear . . . ?"

"My mother called."

They sat on the edge of Shelley's cot and held each other and wept.

Within the week, Shelley was listed as "problem: behavior uncontrollable."

After Deedee's suicide her trancelike state was broken. A fury seized her mind and her soul. She felt she could go mad, trying to fathom just what Deedee had done that was so criminal she had to be destroyed in this way. Their lives had touched. They had been like sisters, protective of each other. They had known each other's days of desperation and of hope. Shelley began to feel that she could kill.

She felt detached from all the others. She had a sense of death all around her now. When she slept, she would wake up shaking with a kind of fever. Sometimes when she woke up she was sobbing. In the dark cell, no one heard and no one came. In a way she was glad of that; she knew that she had to strike back at something or someone. In class she refused to cooperate, slumped silently in her chair, the rage boiling up without outlet.

Christine's chair stood empty. Christine had been allowed home on a two-day pass, accompanied by a guard in plainclothes not to attract attention, to attend Deedee's funeral. Shelley wasn't allowed the privilege; she "wasn't a member of the family." She was at breaking point.

At meals she picked at the food. She was edgy and knew she couldn't trust her emotions. When the officer on duty began to insist at lunch that she finish "that good pork chop," Shelley replied by sweeping her plate and every other girl's plate within reach off the table.

"Lay off me, you goddam motherfucker!" she screamed.

The guard forced Shelley's arms behind her back and dragged her away from the table. The other girls clumped together in fear, or shrieked with excitement at the break in routine.

Shelley was pulled and shoved all the way to her room, and locked in. She went on a rampage, cursing and yelling, pulling her cot apart, tearing the sheet in little bits and pieces, throwing books around, throwing her shoes at the peephole. She rampaged for a long time before she threw herself in a corner, pulling her knees up to her chin, feeling spent and terrified. Terrified of her inner rage and of what they'd do to her.

The nurse came. She talked in soft tones. She urged a sedative in juice down Shelley's throat. She stayed awhile. She straightened the mattress on the cot and sat on it, silent, composed. Shelley said nothing. But she was aware she was sharing the silence with someone, and it seemed to exert control, too. Quietly the nurse left.

"That bitch is crazy, driving all of us crazy," Shelley heard the housemother complain to the nurse.

"Wrong," the nurse said. "She's having an extreme re-action to her friend's suicide. She's normal."

Normal. She wasn't mad, then.

Exhausted, she slept.

The sedative put her out for hours. When she awoke, she felt the rage and terror mounting again. She tried to will herself back to sleep.

Sleep.

Forget.

Don't wake up yet.

Oh, God . . . !

Deedee . . . !

Oh, God, how could You?

Why did You let it happen?

For the first time since her transfer to the Extension, she faced the prospect of being locked up for eighteen months, two years maybe, more if they liked. She was powerless. And she was nothing, she told herself, if she couldn't be free.

What was her crime, anyway? No one explained. No one listened.

Girls were supposed to "grow" here. Grow into what?

Must get free of the mood or I'll kill . . . Head hurts too much.

Maybe if I try writing it down. Figure out what's happening to me, in my own words. Maybe that'll help.

She rapped on the cell door for the hack. On and off, she rapped for a long time. After twenty minutes the guard came.

"Bathroom," Shelley said.

The guard unlocked the door.

"Has my case with my cosmetics and writing pad and things come over from Rip Van Winkle?"

"Thought you wanted the bathroom."

"It was supposed to come over with me."

"Bathroom or not?"

"Yeah, bathroom, but"—Shelley was breathing hard again, trying to keep control—"I wanna know . . ."

"It came."

"Well, I need it."

"No way."

"It's mine! What d'ya mean no way?"

"When you deserve it, you'll have it!"

"Goddam you, I want it now!"

"Just shut up!"

"It belongs to me. I need it!"

"I've had enough of this, bitch!"

"It's mine . . . bitch! I've gotta write, *do* something in here . . . !"

"Do nothin', you listen to me!" The guard's face was furious. She didn't have to take anything from this foul-mouthed delinquent. She'd been a problem at Rip Van Winkle, running three times, and the commotion in mess hall had upset the other girls. She dangled her keys imperiously. "Back in your room!"

The hack's face was very close, and all of Shelley's rage began to focus on her. Suddenly Shelley found it wasn't hard to hate her.

She hit the guard once, across the mouth, the way Cal and Cowpoke had hit her. All her rage and hatred was behind the blow, which staggered the woman against the wall.

Hitting Mama . . . killing Mama . . . !

Pressing her keys like a weapon against Shelley's face, the hack threw Shelley into the cell and locked it.

Within the hour Shelley was taken from her cell to a "quiet room."

It was worse than anything she had ever known or imagined. It was like drawing death in with her.

chapter 13

THE EXTENSION CENTER FOR GIRLS

<u>ANNUAL</u> <u>REPORT</u>

...so that in this "close security"
institution, for the most disturbed
girls in the training school system,
discipline is handled as a <u>positive</u>
part of treatment. It is designed to
reeducate and help our youth develop a
new value system....

The "quiet room" seemed to be saying, I've got you good now, Shelley, forget the world, it's forgotten you, face the wall, face the wall . . .

Wall was what the five-by-eight-foot rectangular, barred cell, stripped of furniture and adornments, had plenty of. It was made of grayish cinder block; the floor was bare; there was not even a bed or cot. A pinewood platform extending from a side wall served as bed and desk and chair. The platform had no mattress or blankets, and no pillow (to preclude destruction) during the day; two blankets were provided at night. No books or reading matter allowed. No writing allowed. No clothes—other than the pajamas in which she was transferred. Nothing to hear or listen to, except perhaps the sound of a girl's voice—her own.

During the first three days of solitary, the director came. He was a slight, iron-jawed man with steady blue eyes and a military-straight spine. He had a degree in sociology. Staff was regularly reminded of the joy he found in his own four children, aged six to nineteen, the oldest of whom was studying for the ministry.

"Now this is not isolation," he told Shelley. "It's our 'quiet room' . . ."

"Ours!"

". . . so we can consider our actions and take some responsibility for them. You're sixteen, and you know you've been in a lot of trouble."

"You goddam shit!" Shelley screamed. "Don't hand me

your crap about 'our' quiet room and 'our' actions. *I* want out!"

"Not until you consider what you've done . . ."

"You're . . . you're violating my civil rights!" she shouted. "I only wanted what belonged to me!"

". . . and apologize to matron."

"Never, never, never!"

"Think it over."

"You're like all the rest. Not listening!"

"You've shown you can't handle an open setting, or the Extension. Until you show some control . . ."

Shelley shrank back.

"Now what're you planning?"

"We do have one last resort, but I hope I don't have to use it."

"What're you goddam bastards planning to do? I wanna know!" she yelled.

He stared at her, hesitating whether to level with her or not. But after all, he had fifty-nine other adolescents to consider, and Shelley's disruptive behavior could infect the whole institution.

"We have the option," he said in a firm tone, "to recommend your transfer to a mental institution."

"You would do that?" It was Shelley's turn to stare.

"We will, if we have to."

"You think . . . I'm mental?"

"We're trying to be helpful . . . but if you won't apologize and try to control yourself . . ."

"You'll never get away with it!"

"Your behavior has been diagnosed . . ."

"Fuck your diagnosis!"

He threw out his hands in resignation. "Think it over, Shelley. Apologize and . . ."

"Never!"

". . . show some control. Staff feels you shouldn't rejoin the rest of the girls unless you come to your senses."

"Staff feels . . . what about how I feel?"

"Think it over, girl."

Her meals were brought to the cell.

At night she got the blankets.

She could rap on the door after meals and once at night to go to the bathroom, with an escort.

She was escorted to showers in the same way.

She only got out of her pajamas for showers.

She kept count of the days but lost track of time.

Now and then she could hear, from far off, the sounds of voices and a radio.

She was scared of the long silences and her terrible aloneness. But she wouldn't break.

Once the nurse came to check her health and give her some aspirin. The attendant had relayed that she complained of headaches. It was the same nurse who'd been human to her before.

"Get it over with, child," the nurse told her. "What the hell. Give them the satisfaction."

"No. It's all mixed up with Deedee."

"Saying you'll behave better will get you out of here."

"Can't let them break me. But . . . thanks."

"For what?"

"Being human."

The nurse put her arm around Shelley. "I don't believe in this goddam isolation."

On the thirteenth day, the Extension's staff experienced a violent shock. Judge Evelyn Davis paid an unexpected call at the institution.

A small, pert, middle-aged mother, Judge Davis was known as a maverick of the bench. With her lively black eyes, short black hair, and horn-rimmed glasses perched more often on her forehead than her nose, she looked her part—a strong-minded civil libertarian whose reputation marched before her. She had organized a local chapter of Women's Strike for Peace, and she was proud of her daughter's consciousness-raising group in college, which she sometimes attended.

Her male counterparts on the Family Court bench respected her (she had started her training as a law clerk to a United States Supreme Court justice). But conservatives all, the men were bothered by her liberal politics and her active work in the women's movement. Judge Davis was well aware that behind her back, out of their male resentment, they called her Black-Belt Davis, though she knew nothing of karate and hated violence.

Her initial inquiries on arriving at the Extension were routine. She had come, she told the director, because judges were now expected to visit the detention and prison center to which girls and boys were sentenced.

"Sent for rehabilitation," the director chided her gently.

"Okay, sent for treatment and help."

She'd chosen the Extension, among others, for such a visit—but also because she had recently been involved in the inquest of the suicide of a girl whose sister, Christine, had just returned to the Extension.

The director applauded the judge's visit: "I wish more judges and district attorneys, too, had your initiative," he said earnestly. He did wish, however, that she'd given the institution some notice of her coming, so he could have had current statistics of "intake" and "outgo" and "aftercare," etcetera, to show her, and prepared both staff and girls for the distinguished visitor.

"Not at all," the little judge said crisply. "This is the best kind of visit. Spontaneous. No red-carpet treatment. See the situation as it exists."

She was taken first on a tour of the Extension.

She took copious notes. If she felt less than buoyed by the high wall, the bars, the peepholes in doors, the maximum-security precautions for three-score adolescent girls, she veiled her feelings. She listened to staff. She listened to girls, in class, in the corridors, at mealtime. Her ballpoint pen was busy filling the blue-lined stenographer's notebook she'd borrowed that morning from her secretary.

It was at lunch, sitting with the director, the nurse, and a couple of girls soon to be paroled, that Judge Davis dropped the bombshell.

"Now I would like to see Shelley Clark. I have something for her."

The silence at the white-clothed table with its vase of field flowers was, the judge recalled later, "death-like."

"Afraid that's not possible," the director said at last.

"Really? Why?"

"She's . . . not here."

"Where is she, then?"

"I mean, she's not in this wing."

"Well, that's okay." The judge waited.

"She's been a behavior problem."

"Oh?"

"She's in the quiet room."

"Quiet room? What's that?"

"Just a room where . . ."

"It's solitary," the nurse said quietly.

"Stripped room!" a coming parolee piped up.

"You . . . have solitary here?" the judge asked.

"It's a place that gives a girl the opportunity to reflect on . . . her behavior."

"Can she be brought from the, uh, quiet room?"

"It's against the institution's rules."

"Why, is she sick?"

"No."

"Then let's have her in."

"Now, Judge, really, with all respect, we do have rules, you know."

"And, sir, I have made a request. I request you to produce Shelley Clark. She went through my court, though I didn't sit on her case."

"I'm sorry."

"Very well. Take me to her. You have a rule about that?"

"No, ma'am."

The director's iron jaw was set like a battleship's prow. His face was as white as the tablecloth.

Director and judge rose. He led the way, insisting that the others remain and finish their lunch.

They proceeded, now in absolute silence, down the long hospital-manicured corridors, turning a corner here and there on the way to the isolation wing.

The officer of the day sprang to her feet at their arrival. At the director's nod, she went to open Shelley's cell.

It had been a dark day, and little light penetrated the cell. The judge accustomed her eyes to the dark.

She was always to remember the details of those first moments: The peephole on the door. The stark interior. The bars. The deliberate hurt induced by the walled-in room. A girl, spread-eagled on a bare wooden shelf, like the shelf built in her garage at home for garden hose and tools. The girl's long blonde hair like a veil over her face and shoulders. Her pajama-clad body stiff with tension.

"Get up, Shelley," said the director.

The girl didn't move.

"You have a visitor, Shelley."

The girl muttered something.

"Now come along."

Her muttering could be made out. "Won't apologize. Go away."

"Goddammit!" the judge exploded. "What's this girl, or any girl, doing in a place like this? What're you trying to prove?"

The director glared at the judge.

"How long's she been here?"

"Some . . . days."

"How many?"

"I'll have to check."

"Don't you know, goddammit!"

Judge Davis stared the man down with the wrath of Moses, or as though from her high bench back in the courtroom, demanding answers to direct questions. She hadn't earned her nickname for nothing, the director thought uneasily.

He flinched and began to walk out of the cell. He wasn't subject to her jurisdiction in this institution, and she damn well knew it—no matter how she tried to pull rank. This was a state institution; he was responsible only to state correction officials, not to a lower-court judge. The state officials set policy; they approved the rules and regulations he set to implement state policy.

Every institution in the state used solitary as a last resort for its ungovernables, be they adult or juvenile. Albany officials expected the administrators of the various institutions to use not only their power but also their heads in keeping disturbed and criminal inmates under control. And he was no ordinary warden. Didn't Black-Belt Davis know that he'd earned a degree in sociology, and had children of his own?

He was so deep into his sense of outrage at the judge's manner that he was startled at her new question:

"Would you do this to your own child?" she barked at him.

He didn't reply.

He waited silently for her at the door. He was badly shaken by her barrage, which he fully intended to report to Albany. Summoning his decorum, he decided not to react to her needling. "Seen enough, Judge?"

"Certainly not!"

Shelley was coming fully awake.

The past twenty-four hours had been her worst. She hadn't moved from the shelf. She had refused food for so long that she felt weak. The last tray with its cup of soup, hamburger, and milk was untouched on the floor under her shelf. She felt deeply tired and hopeless. But one word had penetrated her senses.

She raised herself on one elbow. Brushed her hair from her eyes. Looked at the little woman, close beside her, staring at her with warm, moist eyes. "You really a *judge?*"

"Yes, Shelley, I am."

"Thirteen days."

"You mean . . .?"

"I been here thirteen days. This my thirteenth."

Slowly, feeling nauseous from the pain in her body and head, Shelley drew herself up. She leaned a moment against the wall, on which she had scratched a mark for each day. She let herself off the platform, stood in pajamas facing the judge.

"No visitors till you came in. No books. No writing. No clothes. Nothing to read . . . that's the worst."

The words poured out, low and monotonous.

"You come to get me outa here, Judge?"

"Get your clothes on, Shelley."

"Told ya. I've got no clothes. This is all I been wearing for thirteen days."

"Get her clothes!" Judge Davis barked to no one in particular. Her eyes never left the girl.

The attendant, flustered, stared from judge to director. She made no move.

"With all respect, Judge," the director said through his teeth, "I think we should talk . . . out here."

"Just a minute, Shelley."

The judge stepped into the corridor, making sure that the cell door remained open and that Shelley could hear them.

"As you know," the director said, struggling to retain his composure, "the Extension, like every other institution, has its rules. They can't be gainsaid by every visitor . . . and," he went on grimly, *"do-gooder* who comes into it. If you want the rules changed, and the status of this particular inmate changed, you certainly know how to go through channels. That's your prerogative."

"Damn right, that's my prerogative. I'll tell you what else I'll do. I'll have a lawyer on this case by morning."

"Very well," the director said grimly.

"Civil Liberties Union man, if I can reach him. He'll not only ask for the release of this 'particular inmate,' but, on my orders, he'll be told to investigate whether her rights have been violated by your so-called rules."

"Very well."

"And," the judge went on, ignoring the cynical interruptions, "whether this condition in here—in your 'quiet room'—constitutes 'cruel and unusual punishment.' How's that for openers . . . sir?" she said.

Shelley had come to the doorway. She stared at the judge, and she felt some of the hurt and rage and weakness drain away. She wasn't clear about the exchange. She only knew that this woman was on her side, and wanted to do something for her and not against her.

Listen to her.

What was it the judge had said: Would you do this to your own child?

"You got children?" she suddenly asked the judge.

Judge Davis left off glaring at the director. Her face and tone softened. "My daughter's in college. She's crazy for books, too, Shelley."

The judge had become in the instant an astonishingly different person, soft-spoken, motherly, reflective, as though she loved her daughter.

"You gonna get me outa here, Judge?"

"I am."

"When?"

"By tonight or tomorrow, I hope."

The judge turned back to the director. She phrased her words now in her most judicial tones.

"Meantime, as a judge of the court which placed this juvenile," she told him, "I am asking you to remove her instantly from solitary confinement. You are being asked to give her back her clothes, her books, her personal belongings. She is to return to her former room until the contemplated legal action is taken. Do I make myself clear?"

"Oh, very clear, Your Honor," the director said icily.

He knew what his own next steps would be: call Albany as soon as the judge was out of the institution and have the girl transferred out altogether. Let Albany take the rap.

If this judge wanted to, she could give the story out to the press, via the Civil Liberties Union lawyer, of course—the sort of story that the press and television relished, since it involved a juvenile runaway. No thank you very much, he told himself grimly. Let Albany handle this hot potato.

State officials had long condoned the "quiet room" concept—and anyway, despite these mollycoddling do-gooders, he believed in its worth. In a quiet room, a girl was expected to reflect quietly on her misdeeds, to take responsibility for her actions, without the tools around for destruction. His children were sent to their rooms, on occasion, to reflect on their behavior. Of course, they were in their own home . . . parents close by . . . radio, television . . . but they needed to be slapped down for their own good, didn't they? He straightened his tie and stood very tall.

"The funny part of all this," Judge Davis said, cutting through his reflections, "is that all I wanted to see Shelley for originally was to give her something that Deedee had left her."

"Deedee . . . you know about Deedee?"

"Yes, Shelley."

"We ran from Rip Van Winkle together."

"I know."

"We had jobs, Judge. We . . . were going to get better ones. We couldn't go home just then." The words poured out in emotional release. Someone was there to listen. "Her mother was so sick, but she sent her money, I saw her send the money. And my mother . . . she's sick, too, real sick, Judge, and her husband is a sonofabitch who keeps having me put away. We didn't do nothing, Judge. Deedee and me—we were going to get real good jobs and send money home. We weren't running. We had jobs. I was planning to go on with school nights, I got books from the library, you understand?"

"Yes."

"And then that sonofabitch, my stepfather, comes in the bar and attacks me, and the cops came, and all they know or care about is that I ran again." Her rage was rising, as she remembered.

"No one cares."

"I care, Shelley," the judge said.

Shelley took a deep breath. "Yeah. That's right."

The judge dug into her handbag. She brought out an envelope with Shelley's name scrawled on it and handed it to Shelley. "Deedee left this for you."

Shelley opened the envelope. It held a small crucifix on a thin chain, and a note. She read it aloud:

"This didn't help after all.
It's yours now, Shelley.
Stay loose.
          Love,
                Deedee."

chapter 14

THE EXTENSION CENTER FOR GIRLS

NOTICE OF TRANSFER

TO: Family Court of the State of New York,
County of New York

FROM: The Director

...in that the Respondent, Shelley
Clark, remains intractable and too
great a behavior problem for the Extension staff, the Director must consider an alternative to the Extension....

The director moved fast.

That evening Shelley was returned to her old room. As a security measure, she was locked in, but her personal belongings including her clothes, cosmetics, suitcase, and books were sent in.

The prison grapevine had already been busy with news of the little judge's tough intervention. A couple of girls bravely stopped by Shelley's door to yell in to her:

"You got it made now!"

"They're takin' you back to the city, Shelley!"

"Jeez, wish it was me!"

"Say bye-bye to old Hard-Rock!"

The moment the judge was gone, the director was on the emergency line to Albany. He put his side of the story into the record; and he announced—without requesting permission—that he was transferring the girl immediately back to the Children's Shelter in Manhattan: "For other placement. This institution can't hold her. Let that bleeding-heart judge have her!"

He noted with satisfaction that Albany promptly approved his decision. In fact, Albany officials were even more sensitive than he about possible repercussions from the curmudgeon's visit. The boys' institution in upper New York had not long before experienced the scandal of a juvenile suicide; they were still smarting from that episode, which had been reported in the papers.

Early next morning Shelley was escorted out the front gate to the transfer car, provided by the Department of

Correction. The drive back to the city was made without a stop.

Shelley didn't mind. She sat alone this time on the back seat, too dazed and excited by the speed of events. Something good was going for her, she felt. She held Deedee's offering in her hand. Now and then she stared at the crucifix, and felt close to Deedee, and let her thoughts out: *Something good going at last, Deedee.*

The judge not only wanted to help her. What was really important, she had the power to help her, Shelley thought. Maybe others in there, too.

What stuck in her mind above everything, though, was the judge's look when she talked about her daughter. It was beautiful, that look of love.

How long, Mama, since I saw that look on your face . . . ?

The car sped quietly into the morning sunshine, and listening to its steady hum, Shelley felt safe. *Going somewhere this time . . . not running . . . not having to run . . .*

She drowsed. Then, letting go, she fell into her first deep, dreamless sleep in a long time.

In Manhattan Shelley was escorted to the judge's private chambers in Family Court. "Chambers," Shelley discovered, was the legal term for a tiny robing room furnished with a desk, chair, file cabinets, and wall calendar. Judge Davis had just come off the bench and was doffing her black robe when Shelley entered the room.

"They acted faster than even I expected," the judge said with a smile that lit up her eyes. "So I've made a tentative plan for you, till I know what's on your mind about your hopes and your future."

Shelley stared at Judge Davis in disbelief. When had anyone asked her about her hopes?

"What's the plan, Judge?"

"How would you like to come home with me for a few days—until we get things sorted out?"

"You mean that?"

"I have a lawyer looking into your case. Will you come?"

"Oh, God, yes."

"Then that's settled."

"Should I call my mother?"

Judge Davis hesitated. "Do you want to, Shelley?"

"I don't think so . . . I mean, not yet."

"Okay."

The judge phoned her aide. "Get the file on Shelley Clark, please. And tell Bernie Delaney we're ready for him."

The aide, a young woman doing her "internship" in Family Court before graduation from law school, laid Shelley's file on the judge's desk. She tossed a smile of encouragement to Shelley as she left.

Shelley looked at the file with fascination and disgust. The large manila folder bulged with legal-size, multicolored documents. Handwritten on long, horizontal lines across the cover were the many dates and places of her "Appearances," "Charges," "Sentences," "Dispositions." Her "Index No." was in the upper left-hand corner, "Father's Name" and "Mother's Name" in the upper right. The "Calendar Dates" and "Dispositions" were written in different-colored ink by the court clerks—red, blue, black —like so many bruises, Shelley thought.

The judge caught her eye, and tapped the file. "Practically your life history in that," she said.

"Maybe my life is just beginning," Shelley replied.

"Good girl," said the judge.

Bernie Delaney came in. He was young and long-haired, with a breezy, confident manner.

"Meet your lawyer," he said, extending his hand to Shelley. "We're not only going to sue the Extension for violating your civil rights by imposing what we call cruel and unusual punishment on you while in their care. We think your case is strong enough for us to try to persuade the legislature to close down all training-school prisons in this state."

"That your plan?" asked Shelley in wonder.

"That's what the State of Massachusetts did," the judge said grimly. "Closed them down. Developed a system of community-based group homes—for girls and boys who couldn't or wouldn't return home."

Delaney nodded approvingly. "I've discussed the whole picture with my chief at the Civil Liberties Union," he went on. "And in our suit for damages for Shelley, we're going after the entire state system of imprisoning juveniles, especially the PINS. The Legal Aid Society is joining our suit. These institutions are really training schools *for* crime. The girls and boys would be no worse off if they were left in their communities, with some sort of professional help."

"You can make me a party to that suit, Bernie. Now, here's Shelley's docket. It gives you all the legal data and personal history . . ." The judge handed Shelley's file to Delaney. "She's coming home with me for a few days, and you can interview her there."

Delaney shot the judge a look of admiration. "I could have bet that's just what you'd do."

"Okay, so you'd have won."

Judge Davis' home in suburban Riverdale was set at the end of a tree-shaded lane. Some Tudor-style houses lined one side of the lane, but the judge drove her old Ford station wagon into the driveway of what she facetiously called "our palace." It looked anything but a palace—a simple two-story frame house gone shabby, with the white paint gray and peeling, and the lawn overgrown with unkempt grass.

Indoors was comfortable, though—book-lined walls, cushioned couches, and well-worn club chairs, and a big ceiling-high fireplace with logs in the grate. Shelley felt withdrawn as she moved around the strange rambling house.

I didn't know people lived like this, she thought. All this space. You can breathe here.

"You'll have Alma's room—my daughter's," the judge was saying crisply. "Upstairs and turn right. Why not take a nap before dinner? I'm going to."

"Yeah, sounds great," Shelley said.

She unpacked in the small, pleasant room, put her books on a shelf near a portable radio, and lay down on the bed with its red gingham spread and matching pillowcase. She looked at the high school and college pennants on the walls and the poster of a pop concert. She heard a bird trilling, and children's voices down in the lane. She felt quiet, safe—for the moment. She tried to turn her mind off the dramatic events of the past twenty-four hours. But they were there, in her mind's eye.

So were the old fears, just below the new feeling of safety. That rap sheet in her docket on the judge's desk— it seemed a mile long. She'd lived a dozen lifetimes since she was ten, when Mama had held her tight.

What would you have done, Mama, if you'd seen me in that prison, and not the judge?

Left me there, Mama?

Left me for them to put me in a mental institution because I wouldn't let them break me?

Know what, Mama?

You wouldn't have lifted a goddam finger. That's what I think.

And you know what else?

They were turning me into a mad animal.

Maybe . . . a killer.

"Shit! Knock it off!" she said out loud, angrily.

She closed her eyes. Sleep wouldn't come, but she let the bird's song and the children's voices dominate, and tried to empty her mind for a little while.

When she went down later, Bernie Delaney had arrived. He began his probe with Shelley. "Forget the file," he advised, as he saw her eyeing it fearfully. "Tell me in your own words: about your home life with your mother and Cal. And go on from there, wherever it takes you. We've got time."

It was easy to cooperate with him. She felt the rapport. But what she respected more was that, like the judge, he had the training and the power to help her. She told him about Mama and the bottle, and Mama and Cal, and why she ran, and the life she ran from at home and in the foster homes and "Centers" and prisons. He took notes on his long legal pad and hardly interrupted. Once, when she got to the part about the butches and the Racket, he put in, "It's the same in the boys' institutions and all through the whole rotten system!"

Dinner at the Davises' was a buffet arrangement— you helped yourself from platters of roast beef and mashed potatoes and salad set out by the part-time maid from the neighborhood. The judge's husband, Louis, was a foot taller than his wife, and as brisk and strong-minded as she. He had his own law firm in Manhattan, and owing to the long hours worked by husband and wife, they met mainly, it would appear, at these dinners and on weekends.

Louis Davis was telling them about a criminal case he was defending which involved a fellow-lawyer, who hadn't paid his taxes or child support. He was separated from his wife and going with another woman "who had expensive tastes."

Judge Davis said caustically that some clients in a situation like that—"and a lawyer, for God's sake!"—hardly deserved defending, or even "the time of day."

"Now you know everyone has the right to a defense," her husband began irritably.

"Oh, Louis, of course I know that! It just makes me mad when a father . . ."

"Especially a lawyer?"

"Yeah, *especially* a lawyer, turns lawbreaker."

"So . . . a defense is his fundamental right, too."

"Sure. But it's also a scandal. Now get on with your coffee!"

The sharpness of the exchange bothered Shelley. She didn't like the way the judge bossed her husband. But in the next moment, she saw the smile that passed between them, which seemed to say that they had their differences but weren't separated by them.

"Cat got your tongue, Shelley?" the judge asked. "Did Bernie talk you out?"

"He wants all the facts, he said."

"You'll get a real defense, Shelley."

"Then that'll be the first time I ever got one," Shelley said abruptly.

Judge and Louis Davis were both staring at her.

"I never had a chance in those courts, I mean," Shelley stammered. "Mama . . . or someone always was putting me away."

"I'm hoping," Judge Davis said, "that you'll relax here, so you and I can have some talks."

"I'll do whatever you want."

"No, Shelley. It's what *you* want."

That touched the right chord in Shelley. She felt the tightness in her throat fade. This judge meant it.

"Okay, Judge, then it's what *I* want."

The talks didn't begin at once. Judge Davis wanted Shelley to taste freedom without restrictions and to feel stronger physically. The house grew less strange in the next few days, and her appetite returned. True, the part-time maid who came to clean up while the Davises were at work seemed wary of her. Had the judge taken in ex-inmates before? Shelley wondered. Had they stolen something, or run away?

Once or twice she even thought of running herself. The uncertainty of her future got on her nerves, and the old obsession—to run—returned. It would have been easy enough, nothing really to stop her, except she had no one to run to. But even in her worst moments, her jangled nerves told her she couldn't do that to the judge and Bernie Delaney. They cared about the damage to her life. That was the key word, she thought—cared.

When did you stop caring, Mama?

Is that what still eats at me?

Is that what stops me now?

She occupied herself with the books, and for hours she worked in the front garden, pulling up weeds and pressing down the soil to even the lawn. She straightened the garage. She looked at the broad shelf in the garage which held the hose and garden tools. It reminded her of the "bed" in the Extension's quiet room.

And she and Judge Davis talked. Or rather, the judge listened mostly while she encouraged Shelley to spill out whatever she wanted. She had studied Shelley's file and didn't want to repeat the questions that Bernie Delaney had put to her. Mostly she wanted to evaluate just how much damage had been done to a young adult whose "criminal career" had begun at age ten as a runaway. Had she been so damaged by the courts and the prison system that she was now a threat to herself or to society?

In their talks, Shelley, she noticed, would sometimes lapse into long, brooding silences, and then would flare up and shoot out sharp retorts laced with obscenities. At least she felt trustful enough with the judge not to hold back the obscenities—or her resentments.

"When I'm old enough," Shelley burst out once, "I'd like to hunt down everybody who ever treated me like an animal and shoot them down like animals!"

"You mean that?" Judge Davis asked coldly.

"No, of course not! It's just that . . . some people shouldn't be allowed to have power over children."

"Over anybody, Shelley. We have to weed them out of the system."

The violence was there, then, pent-up, but it could surface. Was it linked, the judge wondered, to Deedee's suicide? Was Shelley capable of a suicide attempt if things went wrong in the future?

"I think about Deedee a lot," Shelley admitted. "But I'd never do that to myself. Listen, Judge, you know what I want more than anything? To live."

"That's what you can help me to understand, Shelley—how to help you to live, with dignity."

Shelley fell silent. She was grateful to this intense and warmhearted woman, but could she really understand what was bugging her about Mama and Cal and, yeah, the old neighborhood? She heard the judge going on: "The Mayor's Office is experimenting with a new approach—some group homes for girls your age in decent neighborhoods. There are housekeepers in charge, and the girls can go on with school or get jobs. There are trained counselors who come each week . . ."

"Look, Judge Davis," Shelley put in swiftly, "if you really want to help me . . . to help me *live* . . . then no more 'homes,' no more counselors or housekeepers or whatever they call themselves. Please! That's okay for some kids, but it's not my bag, Judge! I've had enough 'homes,' shelters, prisons to last me the rest of my life!"

"Okay, Shelley. So what's the alternative? Let's talk about what we call 'reachable goals.' "

"Reachable goals!

Oh, God, how can I make her understand?

What in hell's a "reachable goal" to me?

Home with Mama?

No more.

Can't trust her.

In fact, I hate to say it, but the hell with you, Mama, and that bastard you live with!

There have to be other ways, I think, than running to death all the time. And, Mama, you're death to me.

That's why I haven't called you.

I want to live, Mama!

"Okay, here's my reachable goal," she told the judge. "I can't live alone in New York yet, because Bernie Delaney tells me there are laws against minors living alone. Anyway, it could be dangerous. So my goal, Judge, please help me . . . what I want is to live with Mrs. Farber on our street—if she'll have me."

"Tell me about Mrs. Farber, Shelley."

So Shelley told the judge, pouring it on to make Mrs. Farber even more of an angel than she had been to her: how Mrs. Sarah Farber looked on her as a daughter— "She told my mother that, Judge"—and how she was kind and didn't pry; and how, since Shelley was ten years old, she'd always felt free to be with Mrs. Farber; and how Mrs. Farber had taken her in when she ran from Rip Van Winkle, without asking questions, and had gone to court even though she'd been powerless to help Shelley, but she'd gone anyway when Mama hadn't even shown up. And, Shelley wound up, exhausted by her recital but desperate to seal her case, "Mrs. Farber's a bit old, but she's just been my best support in life . . . till now."

"Meaning?"

"Meaning," Shelley added quietly, "I have your support, too."

The judge nodded, and fell silent a moment.

"Mrs. Farber sounds like a reasonable goal, Shelley. You'd go back to school?"

"They shouldn't have dragged me off my street! I can try to finish school. I can show them!"

"Show . . . whom?"

"Show them . . . Mama . . . I can make it! No, it's more than that. It's for Deedee, too!"

"That's what you want, for starters?"

"Yes. And Judge Davis"—Shelley struggled to find the right words without giving in to her emotion—"I really do appreciate everything, and I'd like to go on with these talks . . . with you, I mean."

"I want that too, Shelley. Now, I'm going to call Mrs. Farber. If she consents, I can tell you this—the state pays her for your care while you live with her."

"Just for taking me in?"

"She's not just taking you in. It's for the care and food and clothing you'll need, yes, but most of all . . . because you want to be there!"

Oh, Mama, Mama, why couldn't I have gone to Mrs. Farber in the first place . . . years and years ago, before all this rotten filthy business with commitment and prison?

Judge Davis telephoned Mrs. Farber. She briefed her on what had happened to Shelley since her last commitment to the Extension and her release.

Mrs. Farber was awed that a judge was on the phone, intervening directly in Shelley's behalf. But not so awed that she could not be herself. "Just send Shelley to me, Judge, Your Honor," she said. "She's fine with me. Can she come to the phone, please?"

Shelley tried to thank Mrs. Farber, but she cried instead.

"Go on, cry, cry! It's all right, it's good for you," Mrs. Farber said. "When you coming, Shelley?"

chapter 15

Shelley stood on West Eighty-Fourth Street and looked around. So many thoughts flashed through her mind, but one was the strongest: I can look around without being afraid. No one's after me.

It was late morning. The kids were in school, and the street was strangely quiet. Going toward Broadway was a young mother, one hand grasping her toddler, the other her shopping cart. A man walked his dog while reading the paper. For the briefest moment, Shelley stared in the direction of Mama's house. Then she ran up the steps to her new home.

Shelley threw herself into Mrs. Farber's arms, and the friends held each other.

"Your room's all ready, Shelley. Now, how about a . . ."

Shelley anticipated her. ". . . cuppa soup?"

They laughed, and hugged each other again.

Shelley didn't take time to unpack. She wanted to get to school, to re-register, maybe ask about a part-time job, she told Mrs. Farber.

Neither of them mentioned Mama.

In school, Shelley found she had fallen so far behind her peers that she had to go into remedial classes "for all ages." She told herself she didn't care. She was back, and she was free . . . free to advance, too, as fast as she could, she was told. With hard work she might be able to make up for lost time in a year. She had once been in the top third of her class in reading, writing, and history. Math and science were the toughies. She threw

148

herself into her studies with such compulsion now that the dean, duly impressed, soon invited her to help tutor slower students after school in reading. It paid fifty cents an hour, and she was elated.

"I'll get there. I'm a student aide," she joyfully reported to Judge Davis. They were meeting twice a month on Fridays after school. Shelley went by subway to the judge's house, and over a buffet meal at the fireplace, with the house to themselves, she clued the judge into her work and her problems. She still felt a distrust of authority figures—"but not the dean, who's giving me a lot of responsibility," and apparently not the tough little judge.

She told Judge Davis it was hard to avoid her former friends, in school and out, who themselves had been in trouble. She was something of a celebrity now, because the old gang thought her case was "a gas"—a great event —and had been in the newspapers (but not her new home). The gang tried to hook up with her again, and invited her to pot parties.

"I tell them I don't need them, and I really don't want that," Shelley said, "but I don't kid myself either. It's hard to be a loner."

"You'll make better friends. Give it time."

Bernie Delaney warned the press away from Shelley: "She's a minor and needs privacy." His Civil Liberties Union legal staff was suing the State of New York in her behalf, from the governor down to the officials supervising the training schools, for ten thousand dollars. The suit was brought "because of the violation of her civil rights, and visiting on her cruel and unusual punishment while in the care of the state."

Delaney's staff also instituted a federal court proceeding to take away from Family Court itself "the power to incarcerate children who have committed no crimes." Indeed, the state Court of Appeals, in a suit brought by the Legal Aid Society, had just ruled against placing

PINS children in the same institutions as those who were convicted of crimes.

Better to close down the whole training school system, Delaney argued in his brief, in a frank admission to the public that the system *lacked the trained manpower and facilities* to minister to children with psychological and emotional problems; locking children up in barren cells with the rationalization that "we're teaching them a lesson . . . this will help them to change" was nothing less than inhuman. That concept went into his brief:

"All over this state and country, children who have committed no crimes are incarcerated with little or no due process, confined under cruel and coercive conditions, and abused under color of law . . . ."

Judge Davis strongly concurred with the legal and social approach.

And, in her own way, so did Mrs. Farber. "Look, Shelley, I'm not so clever and I haven't had much education," she told Shelley after she returned from one Friday session with the judge, "but I've raised two children who are married and have kids of their own now. And I keep a nice, spotless home, don't I?"

"The best, Mrs. Farber."

"So tell me, why didn't they let you come to me before all the damage was done?" Lines of anger furrowed her brow. "That Welfare woman knew you used to come to me since you were little. You loved to come here, yes, Shelley?"

"Yes."

"Then that's what I don't understand! Why drag you away to those terrible places and lock you up and give you a record . . . for what? What're you supposed to have done, Shelley? Rob a bank?"

"It was Mama and Cal. They could do it to me, under the law, remember?"

"I remember. But what about all those officials . . . they should have brains enough to see you'd be better off right here, on your own street, with me! And . . . and think of all those other girls you been telling me about, thrown out like garbage. There's more damage done to them by now than before they were caught, right?"

"Mrs. Farber, you know what?"

"What, Shelley?"

"I love you, Mrs. Farber."

The angry lines in Mrs. Farber's brow faded. She looked embarrassed but pleased. "That's an answer?" she joked.

That semester was the hardest Shelley could remember. But the headaches were nearly gone, which had to mean something. She stuck close to Mrs. Farber, sometimes went for walks in Central Park with her, did some housework and shopping.

Secretly, she cherished an old fantasy: She would meet Tony, tell him everything, and he'd understand and be friends again. She saw him from a distance occasionally, in the corridor or lunchroom. He was with other boys or a girl usually. He was graduating soon, and, now a basketball star, he was very popular. She'd heard he would enter the University of Notre Dame.

One afternoon, as she walked toward the dean's office to fix her schedule, she saw Tony with a bunch of boys coming in her direction. She stopped and waited. He seemed heavier now, with an athlete's assurance, or so it seemed to her as she admired his rugged good looks. His friends were close replicas of him, wearing their lettered shirts like badges of honor. She stepped in Tony's way.

"Hi, Tony," she said.

"Jeez, it's the Clark broad!" a boy yelled.

"Can you put me in the papers?"

"How about a piece of the action?"

"Where're ya hustling now?"

Shelley fell back, her eyes blazing, the old fury begin-

ning to surface. She tried not to show it. Forget it . . .
stay loose . . . have to stay loose!

"How're you doing, Tony?"

Tony looked confused. He ran a hand through his hair,
shrugged, and gave a short laugh. He kept moving. "I'm
okay, I guess."

"That's good. I thought . . ."

"Gotta run. Practice. See you around, girl."

He hurried on with his pals.

Girl!

She couldn't help it then. She spat it out, after them.
"You bastards!"

They were too far down the corridor to hear it, but
others passing by did. One girl threw Shelley a look of
disgust.

That's okay, baby, I feel the same way.

Disgusted.

With myself mostly.

Still Hard-Rock Hotel inside, I guess.

And that's bad.

She told the judge about the episode the next Friday.
She held nothing back.

"So, you got rid of another fantasy," Judge Davis said
clamly.

"I really wanted to hurt them—physically."

"But you didn't."

"That's right, thank God."

"Talking it out helps?"

"Yeah. It helps a whole lot."

At last, she telephoned Mama.

Mama sounded excited. "I've been reading about you
in the papers, Shelley. They had to spring you after that
judge got interested, didn't they? I told ya, Shelley . . .
only God and six cops, and she's like . . . like God!"

"Yes, Mama."

"Where are you calling from?"

"I'm living with Mrs. Farber."

There was a shocked silence at the other end.

"You here on the street, and you ain't got in touch with me?"

"It's a big neighborhood, Mama. It seemed best for a while."

"Why are you calling me now?"

"Because I'm ready to talk to you now, Mama."

"Oh, you're ready."

"Yes."

"You sound damn calm about it."

"That's right, Mama. Calm."

Another pause. Then Mama's voice, shaken, as though holding back the tears: "When can I see you?"

"After school. Here at Mrs. Farber's."

"I'll come tonight."

"No, Mama, after school, around five o'clock. I don't want your husband to miss you, or you to tell him where I'm living."

"Okay, Shelley."

Mrs. Farber went out before Mama was due: "I'll do the shopping today, honey. There's a nice Danish ring in the cake box, and make coffee." Shelley was grateful for her tact.

She carried the Danish and two mugs for the instant coffee to the small table at the window. The street noises were muffled. She dreaded the coming visit. She looked down on the street that had been her blessing and her bane.

Mama came promptly at five.

Shelley kissed her, but she felt she was kissing a stranger.

Mama had dyed her hair again, a brassy gold. It hung string-straight below her shoulders. Her eyes and mouth were heavily made up. Her ears were hung with loops too large for her thin, seamed face. She wore a short two-piece flowered dress and platform shoes with thick heels. She looked as if she were trying to be twenty.

"Who're you made up for, Mama?"

"Don't be fresh! I thought, you know, there might be a reporter or something. Anyway, Cal likes me to look this way."

They sat at the table, drinking coffee, and Shelley served the Danish.

"Is he good to you, Mama?"

Mama looked puzzled.

"I'm married to him, ain't I?"

"That's not what I asked."

"You got a drink, Shelley?"

"No."

"Gotta have a drink."

"We don't keep any liquor."

Mama drank her coffee.

"You know, we figured, Shelley, that with all that money coming to you . . ."

"We?"

"Well, okay, me . . . I thought when you get that money . . ."

"*If* I get the money. If the lawyer wins my case. He's testing the law just now, he says. The case could take a long time."

"Anyway, I figured it'd look better if you were home, living with us, I mean."

"Never, Mama."

"What d'ya mean, never?"

"I'm never coming home."

"You always wanted to before!"

"That was before."

"Then why'd you call me? Answer me that!"

"I didn't want to bump into you accidentally, on the street or somewhere."

"Why, you little bitch, you didn't really want to see me!"

"You're wrong, Mama. I wanted to see you."

"Then whyn't you come home?"

"Because of the money?"

"Because I need you, baby!"

"You're lying, Mama."

"Where'd you get off, talking like that? Like you hate me!"

Shelley stared at her mother. "Mama, can you try to understand this: I don't know what I feel yet. But I know I won't live with you and that man again. I know it was right for me to run from your house. I've been through hell . . . and I hope I'm finished forever with that hell. But I learned one thing there. It wasn't just Cal, Mama . . . I had to get away from you, too."

"I don't know what you're talking about."

"I didn't really expect you to, Mama."

"Cal's all I've got! I've gotta hang onto Cal!"

"That why you're hitting the bottle so hard?"

"Don't you talk like that! Just need a drink."

"You're lying again, Mama. You need help."

"Look who's talking about help!"

"Right, Mama, I need it. I can't make it alone."

"Well, this conversation's going nowhere. I better be going, Shelley. I'm around . . . if you need me."

"Sure, Mama. Take care."

Mama left the rest of her coffee.

From the window, Shelley watched Mama hurry up the street to the corner bar. She felt an aching pity swell inside her for Mama, but she didn't fool herself. She knew that the feeling didn't come out of love. It hurt her to recognize that.

It suddenly seemed to Shelley, as she cleared the dishes away, that in this bad and painful scene with Mama, she had been the mother and Mama the child.

Not long after Mama's visit, Shelley went back to the West Village to say good-bye to Deedee in her own way.

She had been thinking about it for a long time, and now she put Deedee's gift around her neck and took the subway to Sheridan Square. She slipped into the New Image Bistro.

The men were standing at the smoke-filled counter, three deep, feet on the iron rail, temporarily ignoring their drinks while they looked at the cage. The jukebox blasted out rock rhythms. The cage held a nude girl, gyrating and grinding away, older and more experienced than Deedee. Behind the bar, a skinny barmaid in sweater and jeans was reading a comic book, waiting for the act to be over. It was like watching a rerun of an old newsreel.

Shelley fingered the crucifix. She had intended to look again at the back-room flat which had been hers and Deedee's. But when Charlie spotted her from the other end of the bar, and started toward her in a friendly way, she left before he reached her.

Goodbye, Deedee.

Stay loose.

She walked, rapidly now, to the church. It was very late, but the entrance stood open and she went in. The memories crowded her. The large reception room was empty. Folding chairs were stacked against a wall decorated with poster art of meetings and trips. The lid of the old upright piano was raised, as though waiting.

She was glad of the quiet.

There was one other person besides herself. The black youth was working on some papers. He sat near the wall of the missing. Caretaker for the night?

He looked up from his work, absently at first, then with delight as he recognized Shelley.

"You came back!"

"You know, you never told me your name."

He grinned. "It's Michael Drummond."

"Hi, Michael. I've brought something."

Shelley drew from her pocket a snapshot of herself. It

was one taken by Jeffrey Olsen of each of the Cottage C girls and given to them as souvenirs.

She held it out to Michael.

"If you like, you can put it up with the others," Shelley said, "with a red sticker."

epilogue

FAMILY COURT OF THE STATE OF NEW YORK

COUNTY OF New York . . . .

<u>PRESENT</u>

Hon. Evelyn Davis . . . .
                              Judge

In the matter of

Shelley Clark . . . . **Docket No.** S7352 . . . . .

> ...noted this day that above Respondent
> is attending school in her community
> and is tutoring others. She is resist-
> ant to formal counseling at present,
> but I believe she will accept it after
> several more sessions with me. Shel-
> ley is still distrustful of some author-
> ity figures and potentially violent.
> But I feel she also is making unex-
> pectedly good progress....

More SIGNET Titles You'll Want to Read

☐ **THE LONG ROAD BACK by Eda Franchi.** The true story of a beautiful and brilliant young woman's nightmare struggle against drugs and madness.
(#W6360—$1.50)

☐ **FALLING by Susan Fromberg Schaeffer.** The heart-breaking story of a young woman's fight against a descent into madness. "I love this novel . . . the finest new talent we've seen in a long while."—**New York Times Book Review** (#W5897—$1.50)

☐ **THE SNAKE PIT by Mary Jane Ward.** The dramatic best-seller about a young woman's mental breakdown and her torturous recovery in a state hospital for the insane. (#Y5527—$1.25)

☐ **I NEVER PROMISED YOU A ROSE GARDEN by Joanne Greenberg.** A beautifully written, bestselling novel of rare insight about a young girl's courageous fight to regain her sanity in a mental hospital.
(#Y4835—$1.25)

☐ **LAST SUMMER by Evan Hunter.** By the bestselling author of **The Blackboard Jungle**, this is a shocking yet tender look at the world of three teenagers and their boredom which leads them from beer drinking to the rape of a young girl. (#Y5587—$1.25)